## *A reality show's wacky challenge goes very wrong ...*

I kicked hard, my hands stretched out, groping for the bottom of the pool. Even now that I was down in the "water," I couldn't see the bottom. My fingers brushed against something smooth. A plate. I snatched it up and felt for more. I found a glass next.

But plates should be easier to carry. With luck, I could get a stack of them before I had to surface for air. My lungs were already starting to burn a little. I did some more feeling around. Got another plate. Yeah!

*Just a couple more, then air,* I told my lungs. I held my plates close to my body with one hand, and swept the other hand in a wide arc. I wanted to cover area fast. My forearm hit something. It wasn't as hard as a plate or a glass, though.

I moved my hand back and took another feel. Now I found a hard part. But small. Way too small. And surrounded by softness.

My lungs were on fire. But I had to see if I was right. I didn't want to be right.

I pulled myself closer to the thing at the bottom of the pool.

It was a body.

# THE HARDY BOYS

### Undercover Brothers®

**Available from Simon & Schuster**

# THE HARDY BOYS

Undercover Brothers®

## FRANKLIN W. DIXON

## #22 Deprivation House

**Aladdin Paperbacks**
**New York   London   Toronto   Sydney**

ALADDIN PAPERBACKS
An imprint of Simon & Schuster Children's Publishing Division
1230 Avenue of the Americas, New York, NY 10020
Copyright © 2008 by Simon & Schuster, Inc.
All rights reserved, including the right of reproduction in whole or in part in any form.
THE HARDY BOYS MYSTERY STORIES and HARDY BOYS UNDER-COVER BROTHERS are registered trademarks of Simon & Schuster, Inc.
ALADDIN PAPERBACKS and related logo are registered trademarks of Simon & Schuster, Inc.
Designed by Lisa Vega
The text of this book was set in Aldine 401 BT.
Manufactured in the United States of America
First Aladdin Paperbacks edition May 2008
10 9 8 7 6 5 4 3 2 1
Library of Congress Control Number 2008920164
ISBN-13: 978-1-4169-6170-3
ISBN-10: 1-4169-6170-4

# TABLE OF CONTENTS

## Avalanche!

**F**rank and I carefully picked our way through the cave. The walls glowed with ghostly green phosphorescence. The eerie light made my brother look like a stranger.

I consulted our map. It had taken four days to find someone who would allow us to make a copy with no questions asked. "I think we turn left up here," I said. Frank nodded.

The ground began to quiver beneath our feet. The quiver became a rumble. I looked at Frank. I knew what he was thinking. I was thinking the same thing.

Avalanche!

Boulders the size of Volkswagens tumble around

us. I dove for the cave floor, but I still managed to get smacked by one. It stung, too. The things might have been made of painted Styrofoam, but they were still pretty humongous masses of painted Styrofoam.

I stayed low as the mining cars chugged by on the track. Once they rounded the bend—*slooowly*—the wires holding the "boulders" retracted, pulling them back up to the ceiling. Ready to terrify the next group of kids who dared to get on the Lost Dutchman's Mine Ride. Heh, heh, heh.

I stood up once I was sure I couldn't be seen by the kids. I didn't want to spoil the magic.

"I don't know why you thought we needed a map, anyway. This place is about the size of a mini-mart," I complained.

"I want to find the evidence fast and get out of here," Frank told me, shoving himself to his feet. "We don't know how many times the thieves make drops, and I'd rather not run into them if we can help it."

Frank started forward, then made a left. I followed him. We hit a dingy room away from the sight line of the tracks. It was filled with junk that had clearly been part of the ride, but needed repairs.

"You don't think . . . ?" I asked, staring at a wheelbarrow full of chipped "gold nuggets." They all had a lot of white showing through the gold.

"Why not?" Frank asked.

"Because it's so incredibly cheesy," I answered. "Hiding the stuff you steal from tourists with the fake gold."

"Maybe when you work at Frontier Village, the cheesiness rubs off," he suggested. He started unloading Styrofoam chunks.

I spotted something silver partway down. A large lockbox. I tried the lid. Unlocked. Because who would be looking for it in here, back where the props from the ride were repaired?

Frank opened the lid. I immediately recognized several pieces of jewelry. "I don't know why an East Asian diplomat would bring his family here," I said.

"Well, he did. And this hilariously expensive owl pendant was stolen. But now it can be returned to its rightful owner. Case closed." Frank shut the lockbox and picked it up.

"Put it down."

I turned around and saw a guy dressed like a cowboy standing behind me. A sheriff with a handlebar mustache had his back.

"Wait. Isn't it supposed to be, 'Stop right thar, pardner'?" I asked. Sometimes I try to be funny at the wrong times. This was one of them. The cowboy responded to my attempt at humor by sucker punching me in the gut.

"It's over," Frank said. "You've been caught. We know exactly how your operation works. Exactly who's involved. That's how we knew where to find your stash."

"Right," I added, my voice coming in that just-punched woof.

The cowboy and the sheriff moved in on Frank. "Put the box down," the cowboy repeated.

Frank did. Which could only mean one thing.

Fight!

I grabbed a full-size plastic skeleton by the feet. I swung it like it was a baseball bat and the cowboy's head was the ball.

Didn't get a home run. It's hard to hit a homer with a plastic bat. But I did connect.

And now the cowboy was coming at me. That was basically my plan. Why should Frank get to fight *two* guys?

The cowboy gave a quick spin and caught me in the back of the knee with his boot. I stumbled forward. He took advantage of my position and grabbed me in a headlock.

*You want to play that? Okay,* I thought.

I rotated my shoulder and got my arm in front of the cowboy's body. I slid my leg behind both of his.

Then I let myself fall backward, taking him with me. I slammed my elbow into his chest as we hit the ground.

I also leaned my head forward as we were falling. That's important. Otherwise, you can injure the all-important noggin.

Before the cowboy could recover, I twisted around and sat on him. I pressed his forearms to the ground with my hands. He struggled, but I had him pinned.

"Want some of this?" Frank asked. He held up some rope. There's always a bunch of rope around at Frontier Village. I realized he already had the sheriff tied up.

By the time the next mining cars went by the avalanche, we were ready to roll. We loaded cowboy and sheriff on board—the cars don't move at warp speed or anything—and took them to justice.

The lockbox held enough evidence to get them locked away. Heh, heh, heh.

# If You Win, You Lose

Ahh. A little downtime. Signing on as an agent with American Teens Against Crime (ATAC) is basically the coolest thing I've ever done. Knowing that I've helped bring in murderers and thieves and arsonists is a rush. Doing that with an organization my dad started up after he retired is even better.

But once in a while, it's good to be able to kick back in one of my favorite places—the school library. The biggest crime that's going to go down in here is somebody turning a book in late. And that's not my department.

Plus, I'm an information junkie, and this place has all the facts you need. If not in one of the books, then on one of the computers. I—

# JOE

Joe here. You want to know the real reason Frank loves the library so much? It's because he's compulsively organized. I'm talking compulsive as in a psychiatric disorder. His label maker is one of his favorite things in the world. The library, with that whole Dewey decimal system to keep things in order, is paradise for him. Which is pretty pathetic. My paradise would have—

# FRANK

Not in my section, Joe. Out. Anyway, as I was saying, I was hanging out in the library before first period, catching up on some homework. Joe was catching up on some $z$'s.

My neurons started firing a little faster as I spotted a dark-haired guy pushing a cart full of books our way. Vijay Patel. There was only one reason for him to be at our school. We were about to get our next ATAC assignment.

I gave Joe a kick to wake him up. "You're Frank Hardy, right?" Vijay asked. He knows who I am. Vijay's been with ATAC almost as long as Joe and I have. He's one of the intel guys, but he's trying to get moved up to fieldwork.

"That's me," I answered.

"Here's the book you requested." Vijay slapped a

bright blue book down in front of me, then rolled his cart away with a big grin on his face. I knew what the grin was about as soon as I read the book's title: *The Bonehead's Guide to Talking to Girls.*

Joe gave a snort-laugh. "You so need that."

Okay, so I sometimes have a tendency to blush when I'm talking to female types. But blushing is partially controlled by the automatic nervous system, although some volitional somatic control comes into play. So basically, a blush is not completely under the blusher's control. So I decided not to even answer Joe. Sometimes the best thing you can do with my younger brother is ignore him.

I cracked the cover of the book enough to see that the pages had been hollowed out. A game cartridge—our ATAC assignments always came in the form of game cartridges—some cash, and some ID and other background stuff were inside.

"Let's get out of here," I told Joe. He swung his backpack over one shoulder and followed me out of the library, through the quad, and out into the parking lot. I figured we could sit in the car and watch the "game" on Joe's portable player.

"Conrad at three o' clock," Joe warned me.

I adjusted the book Vijay had just given me so the title was absolutely hidden. If Brian Conrad saw it, I'd be hearing about it at least until graduation.

So would everybody else at school. Including the girls I already had enough trouble talking to!

"Thanks," I said as I slid behind the wheel. I flipped Joe the game cartridge and he slid it into the player. We both stared at the blank screen expectantly. Hundred-dollar bills began to float from the top of the screen and land in piles at the bottom. To a *ka-ching, ka-ching* sound, a counter in the lower left tallied up the cash.

"Hello, Mr. Franklin." Joe let out a low whistle when the counter reached $1,000,000.

*"One million dollars could be yours—for living in this Mediterranean villa tucked away in exclusive Beverly Hills,"* a woman's voice purred as the pile of money faded and was replaced by a photo of a mansion.

"Do you think there's a catch?" asked Joe. He scratched his head. "I'm thinkin' maybe there's a catch."

"Maybe one million dollars *could* be yours," I suggested, taking in the fountain out front, the palm trees, the balconies on all levels, the arched doorways, the red tile roofs. "Except there'd still be a catch. That place has to be worth multiple millions. I'm guessing double-digit millions."

*"Send us a tape showing us why you think you're special enough to compete. Teenagers only, please. And don't bother asking for more details. You won't get them."* I could

almost hear the woman smirking as she said that.

*"Thousands of teens sent in tapes,"* the deep voice of our ATAC contact told us. Different views of the mansion flicked across the screen. A massive room with a fireplace big enough to walk into that I thought might be a living room. A home theater. A kitchen that looked like it belonged in a five-star restaurant.

*"Twelve were chosen to live at the villa beginning this weekend,"* our contact continued. *"And at least one of the twelve has received a death threat."*

The screen blackened for a minute, then the *Gossip Tonight* logo flashed on. A film clip of a tall girl strutting down a red carpet started up. Short dress. Big smile.

"The list of people who want her dead has got to be pretty long," Joe commented.

"Why?" I asked. "And who is she anyway?" She looked sort of familiar. And she clearly had fans, but I couldn't come up with a name or what she had fans for.

"Ripley Lansing," Joe answered. He did his trademark my-big-brother-is-a-big-dork eye roll. "Her father's the drummer for Tubskull, and her mom owns some huge makeup company."

*"Ripley Lansing received this letter yesterday,"* our contact went on, without emotion. A piece of deep

red paper filled the game player's screen. Letters from different newspapers and magazines had been glued on to form the message: "You win the $$$. You lose your life."

*"Her parents have requested security at the highest level for Ms. Lansing, so the police have opted to bring in ATAC agents. Your mission is to go undercover as participants in the contest—details will not be available until you arrive at the villa—and find out who has threatened to kill Ms. Lansing. You will also need to determine if any of the other contestants are in danger."*

The screen went blank and stayed blank. That was the only time we'd get our mission info. The cartridge erased itself after it was played once.

Joe picked up the book with the hollowed-out center and started flipping through the other stuff ATAC had sent us. "Tickets to L.A.," he said. "Cash." He raised his eyebrows. "You're not going to believe the cover story they came up with for us. It's like something out of a soap!"

He took a few more moments to scan the material. "Here's the deal. You and I are brothers."

"That *is* hard to believe," I commented. I reached over and brushed what I thought were some dough-nut sprinkles off the front of Joe's shirt.

Joe ignored me. I guess that was only fair. "We got adopted by different families when we were babies," he explained. "We didn't even know about each other until a few months ago. I have really rich parents. Your family's more blue-collar."

"It's pretty extreme. Why do you think ATAC came up with something so out there?" I asked.

"Because they needed to get us on a reality TV show," Joe answered. "Those shows love extreme. Brothers separated as wee infants. One rich. One poor. I bet the producers ate that up with a spoon. I bet they think they'll get tons of drama out of us. Maybe they even think you'll try to beat me up—because I grew up with all the luxuries you never had."

"Have you ever considered the possibility that you watch too much TV?" I asked.

"Have you ever considered the possibility that you don't watch enough?" Joe shot back. "You didn't even know who Ripley Lansing is—and she's at the center of our case."

He had a point. "You said you thought there were a lot of people who would want her dead. Why?"

"So many reasons," Joe answered. "She's stolen boyfriends. She's gotten tons of people fired—everyone from waiters, to a backup singer in her dad's band, to an airline pilot. She's always breaking cameras when people try and take pictures of her. If we googled 'I want Ripley Lansing dead' we'd get enough suspects to keep us working for years."

"At least the note narrowed it down a little. The person who wrote the death threat only wants Ripley dead if she wins the contest money," I reminded him.

"So I'm thinkin' that puts the other people in the contest at the top of the suspect list," said Joe.

"Whoever they are. And whatever the contest turns out to be." All missions start out with a lot of unknowns. But this one had more than usual.

Joe checked our plane tickets. "We'll find out tomorrow. We're flying out in the morning."

The first bell rang. "Right after school we need to strategize on what to tell Mom and Aunt Trudy," I said. Dad, of course, would already know the real deal, since he founded ATAC and everything.

I actually think Mom and Aunt Trudy would be cool with our missions. They'd worry about the danger, yeah. But they would get how important what we do is. They'd get that sometimes there are situations where teenagers are the best undercover operatives possible. But ATAC rules require absolute secrecy, so we have to keep Mom and Aunt T out of the loop.

"No can do," Joe answered. "Right after school I have to do a little shopping." He showed me the envelope full of cash from ATAC.

"Is there some special gear we need?" I asked.

"I'm going undercover as a rich boy. I need to look the part." Joe grinned. "The first piece of equipment I need is a pair of Diesel sunglasses."

I stared at him. "The ones you were drooling over at the mall? The ones that were almost three hundred dollars?"

"Authentic cover can make or break a mission, you know that." Joe slapped me on the shoulder. "Dude, those sunglasses could save our lives!"

"I don't think going on the show is a good idea, boys," Mom told us at dinner. "You've already missed a number of school days this year, and we're not even halfway through."

Mom always has the facts. Maybe it's because she spends so much time in libraries. She works in one, in the reference section.

"I agree," Aunt Trudy said. "Those shows are death traps. People have gotten burned, bitten by snakes . . . I know someone lost a little toe, but I don't remember how. I'm sure that somebody is going to die on one of them soon, right in front of all the people watching at home."

"Aunt T, come on. All the contestants are teen-agers. The producers are going to make extra sure everything we do is safe," Joe answered. "And it's me and Frank. You know we can take care of ourselves."

"Losers, losers, losers," Playback added from the kitchen. Our parrot seems to think he should have a part in every conversation. "Merry Christmas! Ho, ho, ho!"

Dad was the only one staying out of the discussion—for now. Joe and I are always telling him that we want to handle things ourselves, the way any other ATAC agents would have to. Agents whose father didn't start the agency. I think because we say that so much, sometimes he enjoys watching us sweat it out a little.

"Even if you don't die, they'll make you eat something horrible," Aunt Trudy went on. "Like worms. Then you'll come back with . . . with worms. Or parasites. Or some other nasty thing."

I looked over at Mom. "Can we go back to the school issue for a minute?"

She nodded.

"Joe and I have started designing an experiment around the experience of living in the house. We haven't worked out all the details, because we don't know what the specifics of the contest will be. We're definitely going to act as if we come from different socioeconomic backgrounds to see how that effects the judging. And we plan to come up with a few hypotheses on how the other people involved will behave under pressure." That last part was actually entirely true. "Our science and social studies teachers have given us the go-ahead to use the project to get class credit."

"And our English teachers are on board if we keep a journal every day and keep up on the reading. Plus we'll definitely get the assignments for everything else," Joe jumped in. "Even the principal thinks it's cool that the two of us could be on TV representing Bayport. Although we aren't exactly going to be ourselves. We're doing that socio-eco thing."

"I wish we knew more details," said Dad.

I couldn't decide if he was trying to make us sweat some more, or just trying to keep up his own cover of reasonable, concerned father who has no idea ATAC even exists.

"A million dollars could pay for lots o' college," Joe wheedled.

"True," Mom answered. She looked over at Dad. One of those looks that has a whole conversation in it. He gave a small nod. She gave in. "As long as you don't fall behind in school," she added.

"Great!" Joe was on his feet, gathering up dishes— even though no one had quite finished eating. "We're going to bring home the college money for sure," he said over his shoulder as he headed into the kitchen.

I picked up some empty plates and followed him. "You know we can't keep the money even if we win. We're not actually contestants. We're undercover," I reminded Joe, keeping my voice soft.

"Doesn't matter. It's only fair that if we win, we really get the money," Joe insisted.

"How do you figure?" I asked.

"Because if we get killed while we're undercover, we're really going to be dead."

He had a point.

## To Living Through It

I adjusted my new sunglasses and stared at the huge wooden gate. Behind it lay the villa. I felt kind of like I'd stepped into the beginning of the *Willy Wonka* movie. A bunch of other kids and I were standing around waiting to be admitted into a sort of magical world.

I hadn't gotten a chance to suss out all the other golden-ticket holders yet. I'd shared a limo from the airport with my long-lost bro, Frank Dooley, a guy named Bobby T, and a girl who wouldn't say her name—or anything else. I'm talking not one word. Silent Girl just stared out the window the whole way here.

Bobby T talked enough for two people, though. He's a famous blogger. Well, he says he's famous. I've never heard of him. But he claims that World-view Pictures paid serious dough to option his blog so they could make a movie out of it. The option ran out before the movie got made, but he's hoping they'll renew the option and unload another dump truck of cash on him.

It looks like he's spent a big chunk of the cash he already got on hair product. For starters, his hair is mostly blue. And it stands out in all these different directions. It has a finger-in-a-light-socket thing going. That takes some serious mousse or pomade or gel. I know that from an undercover op.

 **FRANK**

Frank here. The undercover op was as a student at Bayport High. His undercover identity: Joe Hardy.

 **JOE**

Out, Frank.

Like I was saying, we were all standing in front of this massive gate. We couldn't see anything of the villa, because there was a wall around the place. While we were waiting for the gate to open, I noticed everybody kept shooting looks at Ripley Lansing. Even Frank—who barely knew who she was.

She was definitely worth looking at. She had super-straight, long, dark brown hair and ice blue eyes. And she had on a short dress, like the one in the clip that was part of our ATAC mission disc. Her legs were long and tan and basically awesome.

One of the guys I hadn't met pointed his camera phone at her. I was sure she was going to grab it and stomp on it, the way she supposedly did anytime anyone tried to take pictures of her.

*Here it comes,* I thought, as I saw her hands clench and the muscles in her neck tighten. But then she tossed her hair and gave a big smile. Huh.

"It's opening," Frank said, pulling my attention away from Ripley. We all had to back up as the tall gate swung wide. A couple of cameramen circled around us to get our reactions as it did.

"Welcome!" a woman in a tight dark blue suit with matching dark blue shoes called out. Her hair was really blond, almost white, and her lipstick was very red. "I'm Veronica Wilmont, and I'll be your host—or maybe headmistress is a better term—while you're living here. I hope you'll consider me a friend, and—"

"I didn't come here to make friends," interrupted a wrestler-looking guy with a skull and crossbones shaved into the back of his short hair.

Veronica raised one eyebrow and looked at him. It was a look that could make icicles grow on your nose hairs. "James Sittenfeld," she finally said.

"That's me," the guy answered, throwing his arms wide.

"I remember your audition tape very well," Veronica told him. "I thought your so-called van-surfing was immature and incredibly dangerous—for yourself and for everyone on the road." She smoothed her already perfectly smooth hair. Her nails were very red too, and so wet-looking, I half expected the polish to wipe off in her hair. Not really, but you know what I mean.

"I didn't want you on the show, but I was over-ruled by the producers," Veronica continued. "They thought you'd be *entertaining*."

"I'll try to be entertaining when I crush everyone and walk away with the million." James winked at her. Veronica did not appear entertained.

This guy really wanted to win. But how bad? Bad enough to send Ripley that death threat?

---

### SUSPECT PROFILE

__Name:__ James Sittenfeld

__Hometown:__ Hunley, Wyoming

__Physical description:__ 5'11", 220 lbs., short hair with skull and crossbones cut into the back.

__Occupation:__ High school student

A girl in an acid yellow T-shirt that said ASK ME ABOUT MY CRIPPLING SHYNESS jumped to the front of the group. "Are we going to take that from him?" she cried. It was like we'd suddenly been transported to a pep rally. "He basically just called us all losers," she added. I noticed she was careful to angle her face toward one of the cameras.

"Not basically," said James. "I *did* just call you losers."

"Well, I'm Kit Elroy," she told him, although she kept looking at the camera. She sucked down a big swallow of coffee from a huge paper cup. "And I am no loser! You better watch out for me!"

"No more interruptions, please!" Veronica called out. "Tonight's agenda is an easy one. Get unpacked.

The bedrooms are upstairs and your room assignments are posted. Then feel free to explore the house. There will be a barbecue by the pool in an hour."

"Is that when we get the deets on the contest?" Bobby T asked.

"No, all you have to do tonight is enjoy yourselves," Veronica answered. "I'll see you tomorrow and explain everything you need to know then."

"Oooh, mysterious," said Bobby T. "I'm going to get a juicy blog entry out of this." He started for the gate.

Veronica held up one hand. "First, a word about cameras. As you can see, you are being filmed now. You need to know that there are also cameras positioned everywhere in the house and grounds."

"Does that include—," Frank began.

"Bathrooms aren't included," she answered. "And, because you are all minors, union rules don't allow you to be on-camera twenty-four hours a day. Simply being on-camera is considered work for you. However, I will not tell you when the cameras will be off."

She smiled her very red smile. "And there are no union rules covering the hours I may watch you." Veronica waved us through the gate. The cameramen stayed close as we entered.

The photo we'd seen of the villa didn't really give

the scope of the place. There were miles of land around it. Not another mansion in sight. I wished Mom and Aunt Trudy could see the garden. It was insane. I don't know if it should even be called a garden. It was too huge. I tried to do a quick inventory as we walked toward the mansion. Palm trees with flowering vines snaking up the trunks. Rose-bushes. And a ton of other flowers and trees. A huge fountain in the center of a courtyard paved with red stones.

"Who has a house like this?" a chubby guy asked. "It looks like it should belong to a movie star."

"That's because it did. Katrina Decter used to live here. I recognized the place as soon as Veronica opened the gate," Kit told him. "This is so creepy."

"Who's Katrina Decter?" asked Frank.

"Why creepy?" I said at the same time.

"I can't believe you haven't heard of her. Every-one in Hollywood thought she was going to be a huge star. I'm named after her. Kit's short for Katrina. My mom and I have watched her movies a million times. I can't afford acting lessons—yet. So that's how I study," Kit answered.

"What's the creepy part?" I asked again.

"Ten years ago, Katrina's husband murdered her. Right in front of their four-year-old daughter. Right in that house." Kit pointed to the villa.

"Whoa," the chubby guy murmured.

"How did he kill her?" Frank said. If he hadn't asked, I would have. It's a detective thing. Doesn't matter if a murder happened ten years ago, we still want the facts.

"If there's a room with a hot tub, I'm gettin' it," James Sittenfeld called over his shoulder before Kit had a chance to answer. He'd reached the front door before anyone else. Big surprise. He jerked it open and rushed in.

"Didn't Veronica say that our assignments would be posted?" the chubby guy asked. He gave a helpless shrug. "I'm thinking if the room that guy wants has the name Mikey Chan on the door, I'm outta luck."

"Let's get up there before he gets too much rearranging done," Frank suggested. He led the way up the S-shaped staircase to the second floor.

*Great*, I thought when I spotted my name on a small cream-colored card on the nearest door—along with James Sittenfeld's. Mikey's name was on there too. And the name Wilson Tarlow. I didn't know who he was yet.

At least Mikey seemed decent. "Hey, roomies," James called out as Mikey and I entered the room. He was stretched out on the king-size bed next to the double doors that led to the balcony. Another king-size bed and a bunk bed filled out the sleeping arrangements.

I turned to Mikey. "Want to wait for the other guy before we—"

"I'm here." A gawky guy with a haircut that showed a little too much ear ambled into the room. We did the introduction thing.

"We were just trying to figure out where we're going to sleep," I told Wilson.

"They were." James crossed his arms under his head and gave an obnoxious sigh of contentment. "I'm good right here. But if you want my advice, I wouldn't put the president of PBOA on the top bunk."

Wilson, Mikey, and I exchanged "huh?" looks.

"Pot-Bellies of America," James explained.

Can I just say—what a complete dillweed.

Deep red flooded from Mikey's neck up to his face. "I'll take the bottom." He grabbed his suitcase from the pile that had been left for us inside the door. Then he got really busy opening it and messing around with his clothes.

"I'll take the top," I offered. "It'll be like camp."

I unloaded my gear as fast as possible. Which is pretty fast. I'm used to packing and unpacking a lot for missions. "Anyone want to go check out the rest of the house?" I asked.

"Sure," said Mikey.

Wilson slid his suitcase under his enormous bed. "I'm in."

I looked over at James. Aunt Trudy and Mom have trained me well.

"I'm not a joiner," he told me.

"Some people think any kind of fraternizing makes you lose your competitive edge," Wilson commented once we were out in the hall. "Think that's Mr. Personality's deal?"

"I think he's more your basic jerk," I answered. "At least he didn't seem too worried about competition downstairs."

"True," Mikey agreed. "So where to first?"

"Wherever the girls are hanging," Wilson said. "That's my real mission. To find a girlfriend. I watch these shows. The people who live these TV show houses are always hooking up. Even on that *Princess and Nerd* one."

I laughed. Wilson didn't. "Seriously?" I asked. "That's your mission? You're saying you don't care about the million bucks?"

"I wouldn't turn it down," Wilson answered. "But I'm here for love. That's even what I said on my audition tape."

I took a peek over the wrought-iron railing. "I see some female types downstairs," I told him.

Wilson shoved his hands through his hair and

straightened his shoulders. "Let's do it." It was like he was about to go into battle and wasn't sure he was coming back.

If Wilson was being honest, he was very low on the list of possible suspects who had sent Ripley the death threat. Of course, people aren't always honest. I wasn't ready to eliminate any of the contestants yet.

"You guys aren't going to believe it!" Kit called to us as we came down the stairs. She took a swig of coffee. "This place has a private screening room. I'm not talking a plasma TV. I mean a real screening room. There's even a little popcorn counter."

It seemed like she'd gotten over feeling creeped out by the house.

"Only four percent of private homes in the United States have a screening room," a girl with a ring on every finger announced. "A real screening room like this—not just a large-screen TV with a great sound system."

"That's Rosemary. She's a mathhead," Kit explained. "She can give you the percentages on anything." She nodded toward a girl in a long, plain skirt and a long-sleeved blouse. "And that's Mary. She's home-schooled."

*Kit might make a good ATAC agent*, I thought. She got information out of people fast.

I introduced the guys, without contributing the info I'd picked up—that Wilson was on the prowl for a girlfriend, and that Mikey seemed basically decent.

Frank bounded up from the basement level of the mansion. "We just found a bowling alley. Four regulation-size lanes."

"Only point six percent of private homes in the United States have a bowling alley. One of them is the White House," Rosemary observed as we went to check it out.

"I bet Ripley Lansing's house is one of the others," said Kit. "I don't understand why she's even on this show. A million dollars is nothing to her. That's probably her weekly allowance. And she's already famous. Being on TV isn't going to give her anything she doesn't already have. Unlike the rest of us."

I was about to answer, but the sight of the bowling alley made me forget everything else for a minute. "Sweet," I said. The lanes were prime. The wood shone. The pins gleamed white. And the balls—a wide selection—looked like they'd never been touched.

"So who's gonna get themselves something like this if they win the million?" Frank asked.

Good question. It might let us know if anybody

here had a really good reason for wanting the money. A reason good enough to kill for.

"Not me," Kit said. "I need the money to stay out here and keep auditioning. If I don't win the cash or get discovered while I'm on the show—"

She paused and scanned the room. Then she waved and smiled as she spotted a small camera mounted in one corner. "I love you, America! And I know you're going to love me, too!" she exclaimed. "Anyway," she added in a more normal voice, "I need money or an acting job when this is over, or my mom says we have to go back to Ann Arbor. We can't afford L.A. anymore. This is my last hope."

---

### SUSPECT PROFILE

**Name:** Kit Elroy

**Hometown:** Ann Arbor, Michigan

**Physical description:** 5'4", 120 lbs., curly black hair brown eyes, star tattoo on left ankle.

**Occupation:** High school student/trying to break into acting.

**Background:** Only child of divorced parents.

**Suspicious behavior:** Dislikes Ripley and doesn't think she should have been allowed on show.

**Suspected of:** Sending death threat to Ripley Lansing

**Possible motive:** Needs the million dollars to afford to stay in L.A. and pursue career.

Her last hope. Not a bad motive.

"I've never actually been bowling," Mary admitted, ducking her head a little.

I wondered how it worked being home-schooled. Did she do any of the usual after-school activities, like bowling or movies? Or did she pretty much stay at home after school too?

"I'm not surprised. I doubt you could lift even one of those dinky purple kiddy balls," James commented, as he and Ripley came up to the group. "What we need to do is cut off some of Mikey's blubber and give it to you," he continued. That way you won't accidentally slide down the drain or anything."

Mary ducked her head again in reply. Mikey opened his mouth, then seemed to decide not to say anything.

"The barbecue is starting up," Ripley said. "Come on out to the pool."

The pool was . . . I know my English teacher wouldn't be happy to hear this, but I don't think I have the words to describe it. Sounds come the closest. Ahhhh. Ooooh. Arhlhg. See, even the regular sounds don't work.

You got waterfalls splashing down these walls of rock. Tiki torches. An underwater cave. Two hot tubs. I gotta stop. Looking at it is making my head explode.

"I can't wait to get in there," a girl said from behind me.

I turned around and smiled. It was automatic. Something about the girl made my smile muscles start working. She was just so cute. She had blond hair that looked really soft. And she had eyebrows that got kind of pointy in the middle. And one of those cute noses that tilts up. She was very cute, okay?

I realized I'd been so busy thinking about how cute she was, that I hadn't responded to what she'd said. Which is a complete Frank move. I have no problem talking to girls.

"Me too," I answered. "I hope we get some swimming time tonight."

She told me her name was Brynn Fulgham. I told her my name was Joe Carr. Since Frank and I were supposed to have been adopted by different families, we had different last names as part of our cover stories.

Ripley came up to us with glasses of champagne on a tray. "Take one," she told us. "We decided we should start things off with a toast. It's just sparkling cider." She smiled. "No underage drinking on TV, right?"

Brynn and I moved closer to the others. "She seems pretty cool," Brynn said softly as Ripley continued passing around the cider. "I'd heard she was—"

"Pretty much of a witch?" I finished for her.

"Yeah," Brynn admitted.

"Guess we'll have to decide for ourselves what everyone is like," I said. I glanced around at all the other contestants. Was one of them really capable of murder?

"So what exactly shall we toast to?" Ripley called when she'd handed out the last glass.

"To crushing you losers!" James yelled.

"To all our loyal viewers!" cried Kit. Not that we actually had any loyal viewers yet.

"To the contest not involving anything that is still wiggling!" Brynn tossed out.

"To it not having to do with small spaces!" added Mikey. "I hate small spaces."

"Big surprise," James muttered.

"To the whole contest being math questions!" Rosemary yelled.

"To anything that doesn't involve spiders," Bobby T contributed. "Especially spiders with hairy legs."

"To living through whatever it is," exclaimed Ripley.

Her words silenced the group.

"To living through whatever it is," everyone repeated.

Well, everyone except freaky Silent Girl.

## The List

"So what do you think of Ripley Lansing?" Olivia Gavener asked softly. She'd caught up to me on the way to the dining room for breakfast.

"I haven't had time to think much about anybody here yet," I answered. It was true. "She seemed pretty nice last night."

"Hmmm," was all Olivia said in response. She took a seat next to Wilson and started to whisper to him. It was clear she was finished talking to me, so I picked a spot with a good view of the grounds. I could just see the edge of the tennis courts in the distance. I definitely wanted the chance to try them out. Except I was here to work.

I studied the people who had gathered at the table

so far—without being too obvious about it. They were all possible suspects. If Ripley won the money, that meant they lost it.

Olivia and Wilson were still whispering. He seemed pretty happy about it.

Hal Sheen, one of my roommates, was sketching in a notebook. I figured he was working out some element of the planet L-62, a planet he was creating step by step. He'd told me a little about it last night. For every decision—such as not having carbon-based life forms—there are millions of consequences.

He planned to use the planet as the setting for a video game. But he couldn't even start plotting it out until he'd figured out every detail of L-62.

Kit and Bobby T were sitting on my left. Everybody else was still upstairs.

"What's up with you guys?" I asked. "Do either of you think you've figured out what we're going to be doing here?" That had been pretty much the only topic of the barbecue.

"I don't even care," Bobby T told me. His eyebrows were blue too. I hadn't noticed that before. "My fans are drooling for my next entry. The whole mystery of it all is making them crazy. I almost got my highest number of hits ever. And you know what that means. Ka-ching. Ka-ching."

"So, Bobby, when the movie option on your blog gets renewed, 'cause I'm sure it will, do you think I could play myself?" Kit asked. "I know no one else could. They aren't actors," she added quickly.

"Ripley was in that Peach Fizz soda commercial," Bobby T reminded her.

"That. That's not acting. That's standing around being famous for being rich and having famous parents." Kit gave a flip of her hand. "Anyway, what do you think? About me playing me?"

"Hollywood likes names, princess," Bobby T told her. "I think they'd be a lot more interested in having Ripley playing Ripley."

"But I'm going to have a name after the show's over," Kit protested. Then she seemed to realize she wasn't getting anywhere. "Maybe you could just mention me in the blog and that I'm looking for an agent."

"Advertising on blogs costs money," Bobby T answered.

"Like you need cash," muttered Kit. She turned to Mary, who'd sat down on her other side.

"I have a valuable product," Bobby T explained to me. "It loses value if I give it away for free."

A waiter showed up and started pouring juice.

"Is there coffee?" Kit asked.

I took the interruption as an opportunity to get

out of the conversation with her and Bobby T and scanned the table again. Pretty much everyone had arrived. Joe was sitting next to Brynn, and he looked pretty happy about it.

"Here comes the big cheese," Mikey said from my right.

I followed his gaze and saw Veronica striding into the room. She wore a deep red suit today with matching shoes. Mom had a suit kind of like it that she called her "power suit." She wore it to meetings when she wanted to get more money for the reference section of the library.

But Veronica's stopped a lot higher than Mom's did. And when Mom wore the suit, she wore shoes with two-inch heels. Veronica's had to be double that, and the heels were thin as pencils.

"I hope everyone slept well," Veronica called out as she sat down at the head of the table. She didn't actually sound like she cared one way or the other.

"I did," James answered. He strolled into the dining room in cutoff sweat pants and a faded T-shirt. I figured he'd slept in them. He definitely hadn't bothered to brush his hair. Everyone else had gotten dressed for the day.

Veronica nodded toward the only empty seat. "You'll be glad you did. In a little while, you'll have your first competition." I could almost feel a current of electricity passing from person to person when she said that.

"But first, I think it's time to explain exactly what kind of show you're on," Veronica continued. "It's called *Deprivation House*."

"Deprivation. Do you even know what that word means?" James asked Ripley. "It means not having everything you want whenever you want it."

Ripley kept her face perfectly blank.

"Very good, James. I wasn't sure if you had attended school," Veronica said. "The purpose of *Deprivation House* is to test how well you can live without luxuries." She gestured to the pool—and a team of workers appeared. Within seconds, they began to drain it. The waterfalls shut off, leaving only a trickle.

Joe made a sound that I can only describe as a whimper. And he thought he was going to win a million.

"Every day, perhaps even multiple times a day, a luxury will be taken away," Veronica continued. "The screening room, billiards room, and bowling alley were sealed last night."

"Like I'm going to miss something I never had," Mikey murmured.

"There will be several competitions during the week. The winner of a competition will get to choose the luxury that is eliminated next." Veronica held out her hand, and a man with a scruffy 'stache began handing out sheets of thick, cream-colored paper.

"Poor kids, having to lounge around an empty pool," he said under his breath.

"And who are you?" Ripley asked sharply. "I like to know people's names," she added much more softly.

"That's Leo. He's one of the production assistants," Veronica answered for him. "He's passing out the list of deprivations you'll be able to choose from if you're a winner."

"Oh, man, junk food is on this list," Mikey whispered. "I need my cheese puffs."

"I wish peanuts were on here," Bobby T said. "I'm allergic to peanuts. Are there any peanuts in any of that stuff?" he asked as waiters began bringing in platters of food. "Even food made in factories where they make food that has peanuts in it?"

"We're aware of your allergy, Bobby. I've given the information to every crew and staff member. You have nothing to worry about," Veronica told him.

"Okay, but in case someone messes up, I always have epinephrine on me. If I have an allergic reaction, you've got to pull it out and give me a shot," he told everyone loudly. "There won't be time to get a doctor. Are you listening, people? I'll die if I don't get the shot."

"Got it," I assured him. Then I skimmed through the list of possible deprivations. Cable TV. All TV. iPods. Washing machine. Grooming products.

"I cannot survive without the Internet," Bobby T protested.

"Then you'll have to try very hard to win all the competitions," Veronica answered. "Remember, if you win, you get to choose the next deprivation. Of course, I'll get to choose some too. But winning is going to help you keep what's most important to you the longest."

Veronica smiled. I'd started having the feeling that she enjoyed making us squirm. "Of course, if any of you becomes too uncomfortable, you can always leave the house—and the contest. In fact, there is even a good-bye bonus of fifty thousand dollars for the first person who voluntarily drops out. Forty thousand for the second. Thirty thousand for the third. Twenty thousand for the fourth. Ten thousand for the fifth. After that, anyone is still free to leave, but there will be no money given."

"Somebody should jump on that," James mumbled, his mouth full of waffle. "Since I'm winning the mil."

"Nobody's going to take fifty thousand when we're competing for a million," Olivia said. There were nods of agreement all around the table.

"We'll see how you feel once you're a little more uncomfortable," Veronica said. "Living without luxuries could be very difficult for some of you." Her eyes drifted to Ripley.

Ripley's lips tightened, but only for a second.

"By the way, this is the last meal that will be prepared and served for you," Veronica added. "You'll have to do your own cooking and cleaning. Unless you want to starve or live in filth."

"How do you decide who gets booted?" Mikey asked.

"Excellent question," Veronica answered. "Each week, a panel of three judges and I will review the tapes from the house cameras. I will give the reports of what I have seen. Then we will decide who has handled their deprivation the worst. That person will then be told, 'You have been deprived of the chance to win one million dollars.'"

"Great line," Kit said. "As long as I don't have to hear it said to me."

Veronica finished her juice. She hadn't taken any food. "Your time is your own until three. Then I expect you to meet me in the great room upstairs"— she smiled wide—"in your bathing suits."

• • •

"Why bathing suits?" Wilson asked when we were all gathered in the massive living room—more like a loft—that afternoon. "The pool's been drained."

"Gotta win," Bobby T was muttering to himself as he paced back and forth behind one of several couches. "No Internet, no blog, no blog, no option renewal. Gotta win."

"Maybe they just want to give our audience something pretty to look at," Kit answered, posing for the closest camera.

Mary, the home-schooled girl, didn't seem to want to be looked at by anybody. She had on a one-piece bathing suit, the kind with a flouncy skirt. And she had a big towel wrapped tightly around her shoulders.

"Guys, be extra careful. Males account for nearly eighty percent of drowning deaths," Rosemary informed us.

Whatever it was we were going to do, I wished we would just go ahead and do it. I hated waiting around. I checked the clock. It was 3:10. Veronica was late.

Joe didn't seem to mind. He and Brynn were hanging out again. She was laughing at something he'd said. Which doesn't necessarily say much for her sense of humor.

"Hello, everyone." Veronica walked into the room, high heels click-clacking on the polished wooden floor. She'd added a tiny apron to her suit and had on a pair of rubber gloves. "How many of you have to do the dishes at home?"

About half the hands went up—including Joe's and mine.

"Well, today everyone's going to get a chance. Without the luxury of fancy dishwashers. And whoever gets the most dishes sparkling clean in fifteen minutes wins today's contest," Veronica announced.

That was it? Washing dishes?

"There's got to be a catch," Joe said. "Nothing's ever that basic on a reality show."

"Follow me, and I'll show you your work space," Veronica said in reply.

I managed to snag Joe as we all trooped downstairs. "Did you notice that finally there's a girl who recognizes the hotter, more happenin' Hardy when she sees him?" he asked, after he'd made sure no one could overhear us. "I don't care what they deprive us of, as long as I can keep Brynn."

"Can you focus?" I asked. "Our mission here isn't for you to get a girlfriend."

Joe grinned. "No, that's Wilson's mission for himself. He figured if he was actually living in a house with girls all day, every day, he'd have to find *looove*. And I saw that Olivia girl whispering to him about some—"

"What I meant by focus was, have you picked up any useful intel?" I interrupted.

"Not yet. Except Kit seems really jealous of Ripley and really needs money to stay in L.A. and keep doing the acting thing," Joe answered.

"I got that too. And not much else yet." We caught up to the others as Veronica led the way outside.

"No," Joe burst out when he saw the pool.

What they'd done to it *was* horrible. It had been refilled with . . . slime is the only word for it. Gray, oily, somewhat sudsy goop.

"There's your sink," Veronica told us. Do I have to say she was smiling?

One of the production assistants began handing out goggles. I appreciated that. The sludge would probably sear off your corneas. And you definitely couldn't see through it.

"The dishes are at the bottom. You have to bring them up and wash them off over there." She gestured toward the row of kiddie pools that had been arranged on a stretch of lawn. They were full of clean water and sponges. One of them had been assigned to each of us. "Your fifteen minutes starts now."

Bobby T bolted for the pool and dove in. James cannonballed after him, landing almost on his head. I shoved on my goggles and went after them. I tried to ignore the feel of the slime sliding into my ears and nose and trying to slip through my clenched lips.

Strategy. I needed strategy. To get the most clean plates, you needed the most plates, period. I decided I'd focus on getting plates first. I'd just dump them into my kiddie pool and go get more. Then I'd wash them all at once. I didn't want all the plates to get grabbed by my competitors.

I kicked hard, my hands stretched out, groping for the bottom of the pool. Even now that I was down in the "water," I couldn't see the bottom. My fingers brushed against something smooth. A plate. I snatched it up and felt for more. I found a glass next.

But plates should be easier to carry. With luck, I could get a stack of them before I had to surface for air. My lungs were already starting to burn a little. I did some more feeling around. Got another plate. Yeah!

*Just a couple more, then air,* I told my lungs. I held my plates close to my body with one hand, and swept the other hand in a wide arc. I wanted to cover area fast. My forearm hit something. It wasn't as hard as a plate or a glass, though.

I moved my hand back and took another feel. Now I found a hard part. But small. Way too small. And surrounded by softness.

My lungs were on fire. But I had to see if I was right. I didn't want to be right.

I pulled myself closer to the thing at the bottom of the pool.

It was a body.

The hard part—its teeth. The softness—its face.

**JOE**

# 5

## o Siren

As soon as I surfaced, I heard a girl scream. I let my plates go and scrambled out of the pool. I yanked off my goggles. They were so coated with gray sludge I couldn't see anything.

I had to blink a few times for my vision to clear. Then I started to run. Frank was hauling a body out of the water. I reached his side in seconds and helped him pull the man out onto the stone walkway.

Frank grabbed a towel from the nearest deck chair and wiped off the man's face. He used his fingers to clean the man's mouth, getting ready to start CPR. I think we both knew it was too late, but that's not a call you're supposed to make. That's for the professionals

"Call 911," I ordered, and I saw one of the PAs pull out a cell. I moved into place to start the chest compressions.

"It's that guy—Leo, the one who gave us the lists of deprivations this morning, right?" someone else—I wasn't sure who—asked.

I let the voices behind me fade out as I concentrated on the cycles of compressions. Frank and I kept at it until the EMTs arrived. They confirmed that Leo was dead.

We all watched in silence as they loaded Leo onto a gurney, covered him from head to toe with a sheet, and rolled him all the way off the grounds, through the gate, and into the waiting ambulance. The ambulance rolled off without a sound. The siren was pointless now.

"All right. That's all for the day. Cameras off everywhere," Veronica finally said. She had her arms wrapped tightly around her body.

"But Veronica, we had that technical problem yesterday, remember?" one of the production assistants said timidly. "We didn't get any of the outdoor footage. Don't we need to make up—"

"I said cameras off everywhere." Veronica shot the PA a how-dare-you-question-me look.

"I thought . . . You said no matter what," the PA stammered, then turned away.

"What about the contest?" James asked. "Are we doing it tomorrow?"

"No," Veronica answered. "I want that pool drained again—now," she snapped to another PA. "We'll move on to a different competition."

"I think I had the most dishes. I'm the only one who got any in a kiddie pool," Bobby T said.

"There's no way that—," James began.

"We'll move on to a different competition tomorrow," Veronica repeated firmly.

"How would you describe the color of his face?" Bobby asked Frank. "You were the closest. You were right down in it. Would you say skim milk—you know how it has that bluish tone almost? Or cottage cheese? It doesn't have to be a food. Just in your own words."

He held his hands poised over the keyboard of his laptop. He was trying to get his blog about Leo's drowning perfect.

We were all hanging out in the great room. We'd just all ended up in there. It didn't seem like anybody wanted to be alone. I'd gotten a fire going in the walk-in-size fireplace. It gets kinda cold at night in L.A., but we didn't really need one. But I'd wanted something to do, and I think people liked it.

"Come on, Frank," Bobby urged.

"Not everybody finds death so exciting," Kit snapped. Her face was still wet with tears. She'd been crying off and on for hours. And a lot of the time, she'd been angled toward the cameras. I think she must have forgotten they were off.

"You're the blogger. You describe it. You weren't *that* far away," Frank said. I could tell he was annoyed. And Frank doesn't get annoyed that often.

"I can't believe he was there the whole time we were in the pool." Mary shivered. "If we'd found him even a minute earlier . . ."

"It wouldn't have made a difference, I'm pretty sure," I told her. "Frank and I did CPR just in case there was any chance to save him, but it seemed like he'd been gone a while."

"So has this made anyone think of taking the fifty thou and leaving?" Olivia asked, looking intently around the room.

James just snorted without looking up from the video game he was playing over in the corner.

"Because of the accident?" said Frank slowly.

It was a pretty weird thing for her to ask.

"Well, it doesn't seem like Deprivation House is exactly the safest place," Olivia answered.

Kit snorted. "It wasn't at all safe for Katrina Decter. Her husband killed her about ten feet away from where you're sitting," she told Olivia.

"Oh, wait. This is *that* house?" Wilson burst out. "My mom's a Trial TV fanatic. This is the one where the little girl had to testify that her mother tried to kill her father and that's why he killed her. The jury decided it was self-defense, right?"

"Yeah," Kit agreed. "There wasn't a ton of evidence proving Katrina attacked her husband. But Anna, their daughter, was a really convincing witness, even though she was so little. She said—"

"Who cares about whatever happened ten years ago?" Olivia interrupted. "I'm worried about what happened today."

"If you're really worried, why don't *you* take the money and leave?" said Bobby T.

Olivia didn't seem to know how to respond to that.

"Are you worried?" I asked Brynn quietly.

She shook her head. She'd actually been one of the calmest people after Leo's body was found. I guess Bobby T was the absolute calmest, so calm he was actually kind of happy, because it was such good blogging material. Frank and I were calm too, but we've had a ton of emergency training.

"I think I'm going to go out on the balcony. Want to come?" she said.

Obviously I did. Frank could keep an ear on the group discussion for motives and clues and all that.

Brynn and I leaned on the railing and stared out into the grounds. Tiny white lights glowed in lots of the trees. "Pretty," I said.

"I guess," Brynn answered. "So what's the opposite of pufferfish?"

"All I can say to that is—huh?" I answered.

"I just want to talk about something completely random," Brynn explained. "Don't you ever want to do that?"

On days that involved dead bodies—yeah.

"Yeah," I answered, leaving out the dead bodies part, since I figured that was the point. "So, pufferfish. They live in water. They get bigger when they're scared. I'm trying to think of something that lives on land and gets smaller when it's scared. A snail, maybe? A turtle?"

"Those can both live in water. Some of them," Brynn said. "You have to be crazier. Like, I don't know, an anorexic elephant."

I laughed. She laughed. It was a good part of a bad day.

I started laughing when I stepped into the shower the next day. It was decorated with tiny silver fish. Which made me think of pufferfish—and Brynn. She had to be the coolest girl I'd ever met.

*Focus on the mission,* a voice in my head said. The voice sounded like Frank.

"Okay, okay," I muttered. I turned on the water and closed my eyes. I did some good thinking that way. The mission. I couldn't come up with any way to connect Leo's death to the threat Ripley had gotten. Everybody in the contest had a motive for sending the threat. A few people were standing out as stronger possibilities. Kit, for one. James definitely seemed like he badly wanted to win. Bobby T's blog would probably be even more popular if he won a reality TV show.

I opened my eyes so I could find the soap. My heart gave a hard double beat.

Blood ran down my body in streaks.

# That's Repulsive

A high, shrill shriek cut through the second-floor. I raced toward the sound. Kit burst out of her room just as I got to the door. "Olivia's bleeding!" she exclaimed. "She's bleeding a ton!"

"What happened? Did she cut herself?" I asked.

"I don't know. She was taking a shower, then she screamed. I went in there and she had blood all over, even in her hair," Kit said in a rush.

"Calm down. I think I know what the deal is. At least part of it," Joe was saying as he strode down the hall toward us. His white terrycloth bathrobe was splotched with red.

"Are you bleeding too?" I demanded.

"No, but I thought I was for a second," Joe

answered. "I need to check out the bathroom in there."

Kit peeked into the room. "It's okay."

Joe and I hurried inside. Ripley and Mary were huddled around Olivia.

"I don't see where the blood is coming from," Ripley told us. "She doesn't seem to be cut or anything."

"I don't think it's actually blood. I think it's Jell-O," Joe answered.

Olivia's eyes widened. She ran her finger over a splotch of red on her arm, then sniffed. "It does smell like Jell-O. I don't . . ." She blinked, like she was having trouble processing the new information.

Joe stepped into the bathroom and unscrewed the showerhead. He held it out to me. "See. There are still some clumps of semidry Jell-O in there."

"So when I turned on the water, it liquefied the Jell-O and then the Jell-O poured down on me," Olivia said from the doorway.

"Yeah. Same thing happened to me in our bathroom." Joe gestured to the red stains on his robe. "There was something else, too." He turned toward the mirror. "You have it too."

I followed his gaze. In the steamy surface of the mirror, five words had been written: YOU STAY, YOU DIE TOO.

"The message was written in soap," Joe explained. "It didn't show up until the mirrors got steamed up."

"Somebody's trying to psych us out. That's what this is," said Olivia. "This is just like the letter I got."

"What letter?" Ripley's voice came out high and thin.

"This stupid letter saying that if I won I'd die," Olivia snapped. "Somebody started playing head games early. Well, Jell-O and dumb threats aren't going to make me drop out."

"I got a letter too," Mary said softly.

"Me too," said Joe. It was true. We'd both had letters being held for us at the L.A. airport.

"I think we need to get the whole group together," I said.

"Not Veronica," Ripley protested.

"No, only the contestants. We'll meet in the biggest bathroom. That way we don't have to worry about the cameras," I explained.

Five minutes later, all fourteen of us were gathered in the bathroom off the other girls' room. We didn't even really have to squeeze. I gave a quick recap. "So who else got one of the letters?"

Turned out everyone had. But I was pretty sure someone in the room was lying. One person didn't get a letter. One person was the one who had sent the letters to the rest of the contestants.

"It's a psych-out. An attempt at a psych-out," Olivia insisted.

"Pathetic," James said. "Anybody who'd launch an attack with strawberry Jell-O and spooky little elementary-school kind of notes isn't anybody to worry about."

"Where did you go to elementary school?" Mikey joked.

"So we just ignore it?" asked Kit. She took a swig of coffee.

"Yeah," Hal answered. He seemed to be ignoring the situation already. He was working away on a schematic of his planet's core.

"It gives me some cool blogging material," Bobby T said. "Except maybe in the blog, I'll say the showerhead was filled with, like, animal blood. That would be more exciting. I wish I'd gotten some photos of one of you all blood-smeared," he added to Joe and Olivia. "I guess you wouldn't want to re-create?"

"Uh, no," Joe said.

"Forget it," Olivia told him.

"Maybe I can Photoshop a picture of me as an illustration." Bobby T closed his eyes as he tried to picture it.

The bathroom door opened. "Here you guys all are." A guy with shaggy blond hair stepped inside. "I'm supposed to give you more towels. You're not all planning to take a bath together or something, are you? Because that would really get the ratings."

"No cameras are allowed in the bathroom," Brynn told him.

"Ah. Didn't know that," he said. "I'm the new guy. Mitch. Just started this morning. I guess someone had to leave unexpectedly."

Had to be Leo. Guess they hadn't wanted to tell the new guy the old guy died.

"So you all get this whole place to yourselves. That's pretty cool." Mitch unloaded the towels into the cabinet.

"Some of the rooms are sealed. The really good ones," Mikey told him. "And Veronica's quarters on the third floor are off-limits. Not that any of us wants to hang with her."

"She does seem a little scary," Mitch agreed. "Oops. Don't tell her I said that, okay?"

He started for the door. "Hey, a tip. No sandals today. And wear long pants." He waved as he headed out of the bathroom.

"What was that about, you think?" Wilson asked.

"I don't know. But I don't trust him," said Olivia.

"Why not?" I asked.

"Because he works for the show. People who work for the show can never be trusted," she answered. "No one can be trusted, really. Someone right in this room could be a plant."

True. Joe and I were. But not in the way Olivia was thinking.

"So you think we shouldn't wear long pants and regular shoes?" Wilson said.

"You'll have to decide that for yourself." She stood up and left the bathroom.

"Seventy-four percent of her statements reflect paranoia," Rosemary observed.

"She's a freak," said James. He stood up. The Silent Girl stood up too.

"So I guess this meeting's over." Kit got to her feet. "I guess I'll go try to prepare for the competition. Which is impossible, since we don't know what it is. I'm just hoping it doesn't involve any dead bodies this time."

A groan went up from the group.

"That's why it's called *Deprivation House*," Veronica said with a smile. "All iPods in the bag, please. As I told you, luxuries will be taken away at least once a day."

Mitch smiled—a sympathetic smile—as he walked around the dining room, holding out a velvet bag for us to put our iPods in. Those of us who had them.

Veronica clapped her hands. "Now, it's time for our competition. As you know, the winner will select one of the luxuries to go. That means the winner will be able to pick something that he or she knows it's possible to live without."

I checked out Veronica's outfit, trying to get an idea what she had in store for us. She had on her apron again. That gave me pretty much nothing. "Today I'm going to put you to work in the kitchen," she announced.

"Unfair. I bet the Amish girl is great at cooking," James burst out.

"She's not Amish. Mary has been home-schooled," Veronica corrected. "And the competition has nothing to do with cooking. No one would want to cook a meal in our kitchen. Not in the state it's in."

Uh-oh. Were we going to have to deal with more slime?

She nodded to Mitch, and he began handing out large glass jars with lids. "The kitchen has been infested with pests. Specifically, cockroaches," Veronica explained. "It's your job to get each and every one of the insects out of there. Whoever collects the most roaches in their jar wins."

"That is so repulsive," Ripley said.

"There's always the option of dropping out. Fifty thousand dollars if you decide to quit—and no touching repulsive bugs," Veronica answered.

Ripley shook her head.

"What are we supposed to use to catch the roaches?" asked Mikey.

"You may use whatever you find in the kitchen," Veronica told him. "And you may start . . . now."

The door to the kitchen was wide. But not wide enough to let fourteen people through at once. There was a lot of pushing and shoving and elbowing as we all charged into the room.

And stopped. Every surface was brown. Living, moving brown. There wasn't an inch that wasn't covered in roaches.

"I hope dead ones count," James said. He stomped to the nearest cabinet, crushing dozens of the bugs as he went. He pulled out a frying pan and got to work.

I though a frying pan was too big. I figured James would lose a lot of the insects when he made the transfer from the pan to the jar. I wanted something smaller. I decided on a large coffee cup and a spatula.

I positioned the cup under the nearest counter, then started sweeping with the spatula.

"I need a new jar!" I heard Bobby T yell before my own jar was even half full.

I picked up my speed. I knew I wasn't here to win a million bucks. But I needed to look like I had a real chance of winning. I wanted to keep myself on the radar of whoever had made the death threats. That could give me and Joe a lot of info.

Plus, I don't really like to lose. Even dumb contests. So I kept my spatula moving. Pretty soon I needed a new jar too.

It took a while, but eventually the crunching and squishing noises petered down. We had to start chasing after the scurrying little bugs that were left.

"I think that might be it," Hal finally said.

"All I want to do is take a shower," Olivia announced. "I don't care if there's Jell-O in there again."

Veronica opened the kitchen door. "It sounds as if you're finished. Use the showers in the pool cabanas like you did last night. You're all filthy. While you wash, we'll be tallying up your totals."

I doubted very much that Veronica was getting anywhere near the jars of roaches. But when we all trooped back into the dining room, she had the results ready. "Congratulations, Bobby T. It seems you have a way with cockroaches," Veronica announced. "You won by more than four hundred of them. Joe, you came in second. And Ripley third."

Bobby T got some "all right's" and "way to go's"

and some applause. James and Olivia didn't join in.

"You'll need to start thinking about what luxury is going to go," Veronica told him. "You don't have to let me know today, though."

"It's not going to be the Internet. I'm sure about that," Bobby T said.

"How do you feel about junk food?" asked Mikey. "And if you're not a fan, what can I do to make you change your mind?"

"Just so you all know, I am accepting bribes," Bobby T announced loudly.

I don't know if he got any actual cash, but Bobby T got a lot of suggestions about luxuries that it would be easy to do without. Everyone had an opinion.

"I'm going to bed. That's the only place where I'll get some peace," Bobby T finally said to everyone that night. Most of us were still hanging out in the great room.

"The next one, I'm going to cream you," James told Bobby T as he left.

"Good night to you, too," answered Bobby T over his shoulder.

Ripley stood up a few minutes later. "I'm going to bed too. I'm wiped out."

"It's exhausting living without staff, isn't it, princess?" James asked.

Ripley's neck muscles tensed. Then she smiled. "Good night to you, too," she said, using Bobby T's line.

I was pretty tired. But I wanted to hear whatever conversation came up. And Joe definitely wasn't going to be any help in that department. He and Brynn were out on the balcony again. They'd only known each other a couple of days, but they were already really tight.

*At least I don't have to listen to him whine about how girls always like me more,* I thought.

"Help!" Ripley shouted from somewhere down the hall. "Help! Bobby's not breathing!"

# 7

## Hardy vs. Hardy

rank and I got to Ripley and Bobby first. Just in time to see Ripley plunge a needle into Bobby's thigh.

"Wait ten seconds before you take it out," I coached her.

Ripley nodded. "I had to do this to my little cousin once. She's allergic to bee stings."

"I'll call 911," Frank said. "Let's all back up and give Bobby some room," he told the others. They'd all followed us into the bedroom.

Bobby drew in a ragged breath. Ripley pulled out the needle. She checked the side of the EpiPen. "I can see the plunger. That means he got a dose of the epinephrine."

"I'm 'kay," Bobby wheezed. "She got . . . in time."
He began massaging the injection site.

"Don't try to talk right now," I told him.

"He didn't actually stop breathing," Ripley explained. "I was heading to my room, and I heard this thump, and I ran in and he was on the floor by his bed, and I panicked. I thought he wasn't breathing, but it was just hard for him."

"He would have stopped if you hadn't acted so fast," I said. "You were awesome."

"Definitely puttin' you in blog," Bobby T gasped.

"Shhh," Ripley said.

When the EMTs rushed into the room, I thought I recognized a couple of them from the night before. It was good to see them do their stuff on someone who was going to make it.

"See you soon, Bobby," I called as they rolled him out of the room on a gurney. Face uncovered.

"That was intense." Wilson dropped down on the floor. Olivia sat next to him and whispered something in his ear. Was he making progress in the girlfriend area? Or was something else going on? I'd have to bring it up with Frank.

"So do you still think the threats are elementary-school stuff?" Mikey asked James.

"What?" James raised his eyebrows.

"What do you mean what?" Mikey replied. "Bobby

T won the contest today. He was ahead yesterday before . . . you know. He was starting to look like a front-runner to win this thing. Then he almost stops breathing. You think that's a coincidence?"

"He has an allergy," said Ripley. "That's why he carries the EpiPen. Because there's always the possibility something like this could happen."

Mitch appeared in the doorway. "Hey, I wanted to see if you're all okay."

"Pretty much," I answered.

"Thanks for the fashion advice this morning," Kit added. She clearly didn't want to get too specific on-camera. Which was smart. Veronica would probably fire Mitch for giving us a heads-up on the roach competition.

"Any time," said Mitch. "There's the stuff for ice cream sundaes downstairs." He winked. "Junk food is still available—for now—and I figured you guys would be too wound up to sleep for a while."

"Want to go get some?" Brynn asked me.

"I'll be down there in a minute. I'm just going to hit the bathroom," I told her.

Frank and I both hung back until the room had emptied out. Then I went into the bathroom. Frank followed me.

"I guess this is the only place to talk the situation

through without possibly ending up on-camera," I said.

"Yeah. I guess it will seem kind of weird. If we were girls, it would make sense we were always hitting the bathroom together," Frank pointed out.

I shrugged. "No choice. So how much time would it take between ingesting something with peanuts in it and an allergic reaction?"

"Bobby T seemed extremely sensitive," Frank answered. "His skin and nail beds were bluish. And you heard him wheezing. He was in anaphylactic shock. I'd think a reaction that strong would have happened almost immediately after he swallowed the peanuts. Fragments of peanuts, more likely."

"But dinner was more than two hours ago," I said. "And no one was eating in the great room. Veronica doesn't like snacking in there."

"Right," Frank agreed. "So what did he eat to cause the reaction?"

"And where did he get it?" I added. "Could someone have slipped him something?"

"You're with Mikey? You think somebody tried to murder Bobby T?" Frank asked.

I held out my arms in a got-me gesture. "I think we have to consider it, don't you?"

Frank nodded. "Let's start searching, working our way out from where he fell," he suggested. "We're thinking there wasn't much time between eating and falling."

"It's going to look pretty strange on the tapes if we start tossing the room," I said.

"Yeah." Frank thought for a moment. "Maybe we can use our cover story. You grew up rich. I grew up not so rich. Maybe I'm not so happy about that. Maybe I don't really like you so much."

"You not like me? Impossible," I joked.

Frank didn't laugh. He has no sense of humor. "Maybe you think I'm jealous. Maybe you think I stole your fancy sunglasses or something."

"Then I start ripping the whole room apart," I finished for him. Then I kicked the bathroom door all the way open and pushed Frank out. This was going to be fun.

"I know you took them!" I shouted. "Where did you stash them?" I gave Frank another push, then dove toward Bobby T's dresser and yanked open the top drawer.

"That's not even my dresser," Frank told me, as I started throwing Bobby T's stuff on the floor, moving from drawer to drawer, trying not to miss anything.

I started checking the floor around Bobby's bed. Frank began loading everything back in the dresser, getting a second look.

Nothing on the floor. I flung the covers off Bobby T's bed and shook them out.

"Idiot, that's not my bed," Frank shouted.

"I'm not an idiot. I go to the best prep school in Connecticut," I yelled back. I hoped I looked furious enough to be out of my head as I patted down Bobby's pillows.

"Well, I go to public school, but I definitely know an idiot when I see one. And I'm looking at one," Frank snapped. "I didn't take your sunglasses. But if it'll make you happy, I'll buy you a new pair."

"With what? Those Diesels are almost three hundred bucks," I told him. I widened my search.

Frank snorted. "You're kidding me. You really are an idiot."

"Hey, look who adopted me and who adopted you," I shot back. "I think my family's a little more high quality."

We managed to keep the argument going until we'd searched the entire room. Me hurling things around. Frank putting them back in place. Finally Frank shoved me back into the bathroom.

"I got nothing," he said.

"Me either." I turned on the cold water and took a drink. Trashing a room is thirsty work. I knocked a couple of toothbrushes into the sink as I lifted my head.

"You don't need to destroy the bathroom, too," Frank told me.

"Actually, it's close enough to the bedroom," I answered. "If Bobby T swallowed something in here, he could have gone into shock and fallen by his bed." I put the toothbrushes back in place.

"Toothbrushes," said Frank.

"Yeah, that's what they are. Toothbrushes. You *did* learn something in public school." I gave him a congratulatory pat on the shoulder.

Frank shrugged my hand off. "Pretty much everyone brushes their teeth at night."

I got it. "So if the toothpaste was somehow contaminated with peanuts . . ."

"It wouldn't take much. Even a little peanut oil would be enough," Frank said.

"How would the perp know which tube was Bobby T's? Do you think someone's been watching him that carefully?" I asked.

"Why not just infect all the tubes? It wouldn't hurt anyone else," Frank answered. "It would only take a dab of oil. You could put it in with an eyedropper. Or dunk a little twist of Kleenex in the oil, then touch it to the paste."

"Pretty genius," I said. Frank frowned. "Evil genius," I corrected myself.

"Let's test the theory," Frank suggested. He took

a small plastic bottle out of his jacket pocket and shook a short, narrow test strip into his palm. He touched the strip to one of the tubes of toothpaste, and we watched as it turned a murky green with a lavender center.

I pulled out my cell, took a picture of the strip, and zapped it off to Vijay with a text that said, GOT PEANUT OIL?

Vijay's fast. He interpreted the colors of the strip in less than a minute. CONFIRMATIVE, he texted back.

I looked at Frank. "So it's confirmative we had an attempted murder tonight."

# Way Too Many Suspects

I stared up at the ceiling. It felt like I was looking at the sky. The scale of the rooms in the villa was massive.

It wasn't the sound of Hal's snores that was keeping me awake. Or even the occasional stink bomb Bobby T emitted, now that he was back home from the hospital safe and sound.

No. The problem was that my mind had gone all hamster on a wheel. Joe and I had confirmed that someone had put peanut oil in Bobby T's toothpaste tonight. Everybody knew about Bobby T's peanut allergy. He'd told all us contestants that eating anything with peanuts could kill him. And Veronica said all the crew and staff knew about the allergy too.

That meant everyone in the house was a suspect. But who had a motive to want Bobby dead?

All the contestants—except me and Joe—had reason to want him out of the way. Like Mikey said, so far Bobby was the front-runner. He'd won the first competition. And he'd been on the way to winning the one that had been . . . interrupted. That made him a threat.

I ran through the contestants. Ripley. Kit. Mikey. Brynn. Mary. James. Olivia. Wilson. Rosemary. Hal. And Silent Girl.

The one who leaped out at me was James. He was so crazy competitive. But any of the others could be as competitive as he was—and want to win as badly. James might just be the only one who couldn't keep his mouth shut about it.

Kit's name popped too. She had a big reason for wanting the money. It would change her life. A million bucks would change anyone's life, but for a lot of people it would mean a lot of cool stuff. For Kit it meant being able to stay in L.A. and keep trying to be an actress—which seemed like the only thing she cared about.

Joe said Wilson came on the show to get a girlfriend. Sending Bobby T into anaphylactic shock wouldn't help with that. But could a girlfriend really be the real reason he was here? There had to be easier ways. Not that I know from experience or anything.

I really didn't get how Ripley would be willing to kill for a million dollars. It seemed like she could buy anything she wanted to right now. She'd definitely shown up with more suitcases than anyone else.

Hal was clearly deeply obsessed with his planet project. Once he got past the planning stages, it would take some serious money to produce the game he wanted to create around L-62. After spending so much time working on the project, the money to make it happen had to be really important to him.

I realized I had no idea what Olivia, Mary, Mikey, Brynn, Rosemary, and Silent Girl wanted to do with the money. Which meant I didn't understand what possible motive any of them might have for trying to kill Bobby T. Man, I didn't even know Silent Girl's name. Joe and I had—

A hand wrapped around my ankle.

I jerked upright—and saw Olivia standing over me. "Frank, I need to talk to you," she whispered. "Meet me in the library." She scurried out of the room.

I got out of bed and pulled on a pair of jeans. I was already wearing a T-shirt. I left the bedroom as quietly as possible.

*What could Olivia want with me?* I wondered as I

headed to the library. I didn't think I'd even had a real one-on-one conversation with her.

"Uh, hi," I said as I stepped into the book-lined room.

Olivia waved me into the chair next to hers. "Don't worry about the cameras. This is one of the times they're off."

"How do you know?" I asked. Veronica had told us the union would only allow us to be filmed a limited amount of hours a day, but that she wasn't going to tell us which hours those would be.

"I have my ways," Olivia answered, all mysterious.

I just looked at her. Sometimes that's a good way to get people to say more.

"Okay, I got Mitch to tell me," Olivia admitted. "He's pretty cool. He told me this was the little girl's bedroom before it got turned into the library. You know, the little girl who saw her father kill her mother. He knows everything about the house."

"So what did you want to talk to me about. Without cameras," I said.

Usually I have this blushing problem around girls. But right now, Olivia didn't feel like a girl to me. She felt like a suspect. Joe calls this feeling his Spidey sense. I call it instinct. Instinct combined with experience.

"It seems like we've got two groups of people

here. People who actually need money. And people who don't," Olivia said. "Like you—what would you do with the money if you won?"

"College," I answered automatically. "Help my parents pay off the house." I go over my cover story a lot so I can answer things right away like that.

Olivia nodded, like she'd guessed something right. "And what about your brother?"

I hesitated. "I don't know. I don't really know him. We kind of just met."

"Yeah. You were adopted by different families. Seeing him with his Diesel shades and his two-hundred-dollar jeans has to be hard," Olivia said. She reached out and touched my hand.

I still kept getting the suspect vibe from her.

"Kind of," I answered, because I figured it was what Frank Dooley would say.

"Joe doesn't need the money. Ripley certainly doesn't—she's just here for PR anyway. James would probably blow it all in six months. And, let's face it, Kit should go back wherever she came from. She's a lousy actress. Have you seen her mugging for the camera? It's embarrassing."

I wanted to ask her what she meant about Ripley being here for PR. That seemed important to the case. But I didn't think Frank Dooley would go there right away.

"That guy Bobby T doesn't need cash, that's for sure," I said. "He got some big bucks when they optioned his blog."

"Yeah, and I was reading on Purple Girl's website that he's already blown it all," Olivia told me. "A guy like that, who can blow a million five—which is what he got—doesn't deserve a second chance. He's not getting the *Deprivation House* money if I can help it."

I couldn't help wondering exactly how far Olivia would go—or had already gone—to make sure Bobby T didn't win.

"Bobby T spent all that money?" I asked. "Is that even humanly possible?"

"Clearly you don't hang around the right humans,"

---

SUSPECT PROFILE

Name: Olivia Gavener

Hometown: Homestead, Florida

Physical description: 5'7", 140 lbs., red hair, freckles, brown eyes.

Occupation: High school student.

Background: Oldest of five kids, helps out family with paycheck from fast-food job.

Olivia answered. "Not that I do." She shook her head. "Or maybe they are the right ones. Just not the rich ones. Anyway, according to Purple Girl, Bobby spent that money and more. He's in debt up to his eyelids."

"Whoa," I said.

"It would be immoral for him or anyone like him to end up with a million dollars," Olivia continued. "That's what I wanted to talk to you about." She leaned closer and lowered her voice. "How would you feel about forming an alliance?"

"An alliance," I repeated. Repeating stuff is also a good way to keep a suspect talking. And I wanted to know as much about what was going on in Olivia's mind as possible.

"I'm thinking me, you, and maybe Wilson—I'm still deciding about him. Maybe even one other person, if there's someone worthy," Olivia went on.

"I think we should include four people, tops. If any one of us wins, we split the money equally."

"Two hundred and fifty thousand each. That's a lot of money," I said.

"I know." Olivia's eyes were shiny with excitement.

"Why'd you decide to ask me?" I said.

"Because of the situation between you and your brother. It's so unfair," she explained. "And because I like how you keep your head in a crisis. You didn't hesitate when you pulled Leo out of the pool. You went into CPR immediately."

"So did Joe," I reminded her.

"Joe." Olivia sneered. "Joe's been eating off a silver platter since birth. He doesn't deserve any more."

"What exactly would I have to do as part of the alliance?" I wanted to know.

"Do your best to win," she told me.

That sounded okay.

"And do your best to make sure that everyone who isn't one of us loses," she added.

I couldn't help wondering if that included murder.


"Scrambled eggs? Plain scrambled eggs? Aren't you supposed to put tomato or mushrooms or spices in them?" Ripley wrinkled her nose as she stared into the frying pan on the stove.

"Watch out, Joe, she's gotten seven chefs fired," Kit said from her perch on the countertop next to the toaster. "Or was it eight, Rip?"

Ripley turned her back on Kit, and I thought I heard her counting to ten under her breath.

"I guess I could put in some of that stuff." Joe pushed the eggs around the pan with the fork. "Except I'm not sure there's time."

"There isn't," I told him. "Another thirty seconds, and you'll have added the fine flavor of charcoal."

Joe pulled the pan off the burner. "I guess we're ready to eat."

"The table's set," Mikey said, joining us in the kitchen. "I hope nobody cares about whether the forks and knives are on the correct side. I can never remember. But I guess there's a fifty percent chance I got it right."

Four pieces of toast popped up, and Kit immediately reloaded the toaster. "Cooking is fun!" She took a big gulp of her coffee.

The timer on the stove went off. I glanced at Ripley. She didn't move. "That's for your Tater Tots." She stared at me blankly for a few seconds. Then she nodded.

"Right. So all I have to do is take them out of the oven, right?" she asked.

"Maybe add a little caviar and parsley," Joe teased.

Ripley narrowed her eyes at him but didn't say anything. She managed to get the Tots out of the oven without hurting herself or anybody else.

"Breakfast!" Kit shouted into the intercom. I wondered if she completely understood the intercom concept. Then she slurped some more coffee, grabbed a plate of toast in each hand, and left for the dining room.

I took the bacon, Joe took the eggs, Ripley took the Tots, Mikey took the juice, and breakfast was served.

"No peanuts, right?" Bobby T asked when he took his seat at the table. He looked good, like he hadn't had a near-death experience last night.

"No peanuts, no peanut oil, no one even said the word peanuts while performing food prep," Joe told him.

"Thanks again for last night," he told Ripley.

"You're welcome," she said.

Had she turned her head a little toward the camera mounted in the corner before she answered? She didn't do it in an obvious Kit-style way. But I thought she might have.

"You cooked these?" Brynn asked Joe, forking some scrambled eggs into her mouth.

"I did," he answered.

She smiled. "You're so talented."

If my brother was a cartoon, he'd have little hearts circling around his read right now. I could see it. There was something about her that just made you want to look and keep on looking.

"The food's a lot better than last night, that's for sure," Wilson commented.

"There was nothing wrong with last night's food," snapped James. He was one of the cooks of last night's food.

"I loaded the dishwasher last night, and approximately forty-three percent of the food was left on the plates," Rosemary volunteered.

"That's because we'd spent the day scooping up cockroaches," Hal protested. He'd also been one of the cooks. "Who could eat after that?"

He had a point.

"The hamburgers were bloody in the middle," Mary said. She gave a little shudder.

"And the frozen french fries—you're not supposed to serve them frozen," Silent Girl said.

Kit pointed at her. "You spoke!"

"I didn't even know you could," Mikey said. "I didn't want to ask in case there was some kind of tragic story."

"Any information you give about yourself can be used against you on these shows. So I decided not to talk. I'm going back to not talking now. Those french fries made me do it," Silent Girl answered.

We all watched her for a few seconds, but she returned to eating. It didn't seem like she had any intention of speaking again.

"Actually, last night's dinner gave me the idea for what luxury I'm having taken away," Bobby T announced.

The room went still.

"I decided to give up hot food," Bobby said. "So no stove or microwave."

"No toaster, no waffle maker," Veronica added, stepping into the room. She had on an emerald green suit today. Short and shiny. Her white-blond hair was in a complicated twist at the back of her head. "No George Foreman grill. No barbecue. No crockpot, no rice cooker, no espresso machine, no coffeemaker, no hot plates, no—"

"Wait! Back it up!" Kit exclaimed. "No coffee-maker?"

"Nothing to make hot food or beverages," Veronica said firmly.

Kit grabbed her coffee cup and drained it. Then she dashed to the kitchen. She returned moments later. "It's already gone!" she burst out.

"Yes, it is," Veronica said with a smile. "Also, the

phones have been removed. I'll need all your cell phones, too."

Mitch appeared with the velvet bag, and we all—well, most of us—began pulling cells from our pockets. I noticed Olivia didn't have one. Wilson either. Bobby T had four.

"What if there's an emergency?" I asked. "I had to use my cell to call 911 for Bobby last night."

"Use the intercom. It reaches my quarters and all the crew and staff's," Veronica answered. "I can see some of you are already feeling frustrated. Now is the perfect time to tell you about the Deprivation Chamber. We've set up a soundproof booth in what used to be the billiard room. If you feel the need to vent about how horrible it is to live without your usual luxuries, just pop into the booth and go ahead."

"But filmed, right?" Olivia asked.

"Of course filmed," Veronica answered. "And anything on film may be used on any of the episodes. But film from the chamber will not be used when the judges and I make our decision each week about who must leave the house."

"Nothing we say in there can be used against us?" James leaned his chair back on two legs and crossed his arms.

"Not a word. Now get back to your breakfasts. It

will be the last hot meal you have for quite a while. Unless anyone would like to take the option to leave today . . ."

No one did.

Veronica left us to ourselves.

"I can't believe you did this to me," Kit told Bobby. "I can't live without coffee. Coffee is my life."

"Drink soda. Soda has caffeine," Joe suggested.

"Caffeine is not coffee," Kit snarled.

Joe held up both hands. "Okay."

"No iPod is a lot worse than no hot food," Brynn commented. "Last night I actually put my pinkies in my ears and hummed. We've been here two days and I'm losing it!"

"You just don't understand," snapped Kit.

She was still complaining when we'd all finished breakfast.

"Hey, Frank," Olivia said when I stood up from the table. "I wanted to get some aspirin from the supply closet, but the shelf it's on is a little too high for me. Will you get it?"

"Sure." I followed her to the walk-in closet.

"No camera in here, either," Olivia said. "I wanted to know if you'd made a decision about the alliance."

"I did. And I'm in," I told her. I thought Olivia

was a strong suspect. The best way to keep a close watch on her was to join her inner circle. If another alliance formed that we needed to investigate, I figured Joe could infiltrate it.

"Great," Olivia told me. "I want you to help me pick the other members. I think we need two. I'm still thinking about Wilson. You talk to as many people as you can and let me know who you think is one of us."

I nodded. Talking to as many people as I could was what I needed to do anyway.

Olivia started for the door. "Oh, you'd better get me the aspirin. I don't want anyone getting suspicious."

I handed her a bottle. "Hey, Olivia," I said, trying to sound as if the thought had just occurred to me. "What's the deal with Ripley? You said she was only on the show for PR."

"You're not going to believe this," Olivia answered. "See, Ripley's parents are really upset about all the bad publicity she's gotten. And you know it's really bad when the drummer for Tubskull thinks it's bad. So they told her that if she didn't change her act and get some good press, they were going to cut her off."

"No money?" It was hard to imagine Ripley with no money.

"Nothing until she gets her inheritance—when she's thirty," said Olivia, sounding really happy. "So she definitely doesn't need to win the million. She already has what she needs to get all the money she wants. She's on a TV show. All she has to do is act basically nice. That will get her the good publicity, and she's golden."

Olivia reached for the door handle. "We can't stay in here together too long. The first rule of forming an alliance is that no one can suspect you of forming an alliance." She hurried out.

I waited a couple of minutes, then left myself. I needed to find Joe. We needed some bathroom time. Or I guess it could be supply closet time now.

It took me a while to track my brother down, but I finally found him sitting by the fountain. With— of course—Brynn. Did I even have a partner on this mission? It didn't exactly feel like it.

"Joe, can I talk to you for a minute?" I called.

"Did you find my sunglasses?" asked Joe. Then he said something softly to Brynn and headed over to me.

I took him into one of the downstairs bathrooms and filled him in on the deal with Olivia. He was way too entertained by her sneaking up to my bed, but he agreed that my joining her alliance was a good call.

He socked me on the shoulder. "If she tries to make you sign something in blood, I'd—"

"Everybody, get up to the living room—great room—whatever. Now!" Kit shouted through the intercom. "Right now!"

# Screaming House

"I think this place should be called Screaming House or Shrieking House instead of Deprivation House," I told Frank as we dashed up the stairs. A few people were ahead of us, a bunch behind.

"What? What?" Mikey burst out. He was one of the first into the great room.

Kit pointed at the plasma screen. On it, Ripley was plunging a needle full of epinephrine into Bobby T's thigh.

"That's our room," exclaimed Hal.

"That's me," Bobby T said, pushing his way to the front of the group.

"What is this?" Brynn asked Kit.

*"Baristas,"* Ripley answered for her. "It's a gossip show."

"It's a gossip show with coffee," Kit corrected. "I figured if I couldn't drink it, it might help to watch other people drink it."

The clip disappeared and was replaced by two twenty-something women standing behind a coffee bar. "That's a Ripley Lansing we haven't seen before," the one with the long brown hair said.

"It seemed like she was thinking about that boy instead of herself," the one with the long blond hair agreed.

"That's not—," Ripley began, then bit her lip.

"What does she mean, 'that boy'?" Bobby T scowled at the screen.

"That boy is actually Bobby T," Long Brown told Long Blond. "He and Ripley are going to be on a new reality show together. They are locked in a house—a villa in Beverly Hills actually—right now. The details are hush-hush. Bobby's saying as much as he can on his blog, but he hasn't said what the show is actually about."

"Huh. So that was Bobby T. I guess he's good with Photoshop. He doesn't look much like the pictures on his blog," Long Blond commented.

James snickered.

"But back to our Ripley. She was like something

out of that doctor show we're addicted to. Young. Beautiful. Saving lives," Long Brown continued.

"She might even get herself off Santa's bad list in time for Christmas," agreed Long Blond.

"Speaking of Santa, did you see that hilarious clip on YouTube?" Long Brown asked.

"How do you think they got that tape?" Wilson said.

"Veronica leaked it to them, of course," answered Olivia.

"At least they mentioned the blog." Bobby T didn't sound happy.

But Ripley had a big smile on her face. I thought about what Frank had told me during our bathroom break. Could Ripley have slipped Bobby T the peanut oil just so she could "save" him?

With cameras everywhere, she could have figured the rescue would get out sooner or later. And Ripley was right there almost at the moment Bobby T ate carpet.

---

SUSPECT PROFILE

Name: Ripley Lansing

Hometown: Malibu, California

Physical description: 5'10", 140 lbs., straight brown hair, blue eyes.

I was liking my theory—and then I remembered that everyone on the show had gotten death threats. Would Ripley have sent them? How would that fit in with a plan to be nice? Threatening people with death was pretty much anti-nice.

Although getting a death threat might get you some sympathy. It definitely worried her parents enough to go to the police, who went to ATAC. Maybe Ripley sent the threat to herself to soften her parents up. She could have sent everyone else threats to confuse things.

I was definitely confused.

"You're still trying to think of the opposite of a pufferfish, aren't you?" Brynn knocked her shoulder against mine.

I realized I'd been spacing. A bunch of people had already left the great room.

"Nah," I told her. "I figured that out last night. It's a salad."

She raised her eyebrows, making the pointy parts more pointy. Would she get mad if I told her she looked sort of like an elf? "A salad," she repeated as we walked out to the balcony. It was starting to become our spot.

"In Japan cooks have to have a license to prepare pufferfish. One little mistake, and you can kill someone," I started to explain. "With salad—"

"No matter how you make it, you're almost never going to kill anybody. Unless *maybe* you don't wash the spinach well enough." Brynn smiled. "That's a very good opposite. You might have a real talent for this."

"It's something I'm going to explore with my guidance counselor," I answered.

Brynn laughed, then braced her hands on the balcony rail and looked down at the grounds. "The fountain is my favorite thing in the whole place," she said.

"I don't think I've even seen the whole place yet," I admitted.

"I'm sure I haven't either. I just make snap judgments," she told me. "Do you think you'd be a different person if you had a completely different past?"

"You want to talk about something random again?" I asked.

"I like random," she admitted. "I like conversations where you have no idea what the other person is going to say. Instead of 'where do you go to school?' kind of things."

"Okay." I thought about her question for a moment. "I think I'd be somewhat different, but not completely different," I said.

"So if you had been adopted by Frank's family and he'd been adopted by yours, you'd have the same personality?" Brynn turned to face me.

"Yeah. I definitely don't think I'd have Frank's personality, if that's what you mean," I answered. "I don't think I'd eat pizza with a knife and fork. I wouldn't have a kitten if somebody put a CD back in the wrong case."

"Frank eats pizza with a knife and fork?" Brynn asked.

Oops. I'd gotten so into talking to Brynn I'd

messed up on the cover story. She made me forget my ATAC training for a second.

"He definitely looks like the kind of guy who would, right? I mean, look at his jeans. I think he irons them. And they're jeans," I said. "But back to your first question, I wouldn't be a guy who ironed, well, anything. But I guess every experience you have changes you somehow. Gives you knowledge. Or memories that are good or bad. Or skills. For example, because I met you, I'm now an opposites master."

I figured I'd given a long enough answer to make her forget my slipup. "What do you think? Would you be totally different if you lived in a different place or had a different family or whatever?"

She shrugged. "Who knows?"

"Fine. You make me give a big, long essay-question answer and you get off with 'who knows,'" I complained.

"You could have said 'who knows,'" Brynn told me. "You could have . . ."

As she continued speaking, a flash of light from among the trees below caught my eye. I tried to pretend I was listening to Brynn as I watched for it to come again. It did. Frank was sending me a signal. A few flashes later and I had it.

Basically, the signal said, "Get to work."

• • •

I wandered around the house, trying to figure out exactly how to get to work. Actually, as far as Frank knew, talking to Brynn could have been working. She could have been giving me insight into the motive of the killer. She wasn't, but he didn't know that.

I heard James's voice in the exercise room and decided to swing in there. He was a suspect who could use some further investigation.

"What's with the blue hair?" James lay on his back on a weight bench. He let out his breath slowly as he lowered a hundred-pound weight to his chest. He looked over at Bobby T, who was pedaling slowly on one of the exercise bikes.

Bobby gave a one-shoulder shrug. "It's a style."

"It's weird." James began lifting the weight again.

"How am I supposed to answer that?" Bobby asked me.

"You're not," said James before I could open my mouth. "You're supposed to tell me to go eat a toad. I knew you were a wimp. I was just verifying."

"A wimp who pretty much beat you in two competitions," Bobby T said. He didn't sound too bothered.

James slammed the weight back on the bar over his head and sat up. "The first one was canceled before it was finished."

"I'll be sure to make that clear in my blog when I write about it," Bobby T answered. "Veronica isn't allowing me to post anything that's directly about the show. Nothing about the contests or that there are even deprivations or anything. I still wrote about Leo, just without the contest part."

Bobby T started pedaling faster. "And I wrote about my near-death experience. Thanks for telling me my lips turned blue and everything, Joe. I put in that we've all gotten death threats, too." He took a swallow from his water bottle.

"Don't you have to have our permission to write about us?" James asked.

"Nope. I'm writing about my life, and you happen to be in it." Bobby T jumped off the bike. "I'm ready to try out the sauna. It should be nice and hot by now. Mitch got it going for me. Who's in?"

"I guess that's the only way you'll work up a sweat. You weren't exactly feeling the burn on that bike," James said. "But my muscles could use some loosening in the sauna."

"Why not?" I came into the gym because I wanted to gather info on potential suspects. I could do that anywhere.

Except what I ended up finding out was something I already knew—saunas are hot. That's pretty much all we said to one another. Variations on "It's hot in here."

"It smells kind of like pine," I commented. Only to say something different.

"It's the wood, genius. It's white pine," James told me.

Note to self: James is not very polite. I leaned my head back against the *white pine* wall and closed my eyes.

"I'm starting to feel sort of like I did last night," Bobby T said.

My eyes snapped open. "You mean before you had the attack?"

"Yeah," he answered. "My chest feels tight."

Frank and I had thrown away the contaminated toothpaste. And anyway, I'd been with Bobby T for about the last half an hour. He hadn't eaten anything. He'd drunk some water—we all had—but his was from the same bottle he'd been using since I came into the gym. He would have had a reaction by now if it was contaminated.

I realized my own chest felt kind of tight. Hot and tight. "It's just from sucking down all this hot, dry air," I said. "I think we should head out."

I stood up, and my brain seemed to do a slow roll inside my head. "We should definitely head out. I'm more dehydrated than I thought." I walked over to the door and grabbed the handle. It didn't move.

I gave the handle a jerk. It still didn't move.

The door didn't have a lock, did it? I slid my hands over it, even though I was sure it didn't.

"What's wrong?" asked Bobby T.

"The door's jammed," I answered.

"Let me do it." James got up, elbowed me aside, and yanked on the door. It didn't open.

"Wait. Are we trapped in here?" Bobby T demanded. He crowded up to the door too.

"Let's discuss it with the heat down," I said. I hurried over to the thermostat. At least this sauna had it inside. I slid my thumb across the wheel.

Jammed.

"No way," said James, looking over at me.

Bobby T groaned. "I finished all my water a little while ago."

"I'm out too," James told us.

"I have about a quarter of a bottle left," I said. I did a quick check of the room. There was no intercom in here.

"Here's my next question." James picked up his empty water bottle and crushed it. "How long can we stay in here without passing out from heatstroke?"

FRANK

# 10

## No Joe

*N*ow where's Joe? I thought.

I bet I knew who he was with, even if I didn't know where. The Brynn thing—it was starting to get a little annoying.

*It's not completely under his control,* I told myself. Attraction and all that released a lot of chemicals into the brain. He was clearly operating while impaired.

But this mission was complicated. There were a ton of suspects. Chemical-soaked or not, I needed my brother.

So I began my search, starting with the top floor. I didn't find Joe up there. But I did find Brynn. Okay, I admit it. I was wrong.

She was standing alone in the library, running

her finger up and down one of the stripes on the wallpaper.

"Can't find anything good to read?" I asked.

"Too many good things. Practically everything. Even new stuff," she said.

"Why wouldn't there be new stuff? This place has the newest everything," I answered.

"I guess I expect libraries like this"—she gave the wheeled ladder a little push—"so-old fashioned looking, to have only old-fashioned books."

I spotted a book I'd liked a lot and pulled it off the shelf. "Have you read *Life of Pi*? I'm usually more of a nonfiction guy, but it was really great."

"I almost always read nonfiction too," Brynn answered. "I just read this one." She slid a book off the shelf—the book that was waiting for me in my living room back home.

"The part where it described the peeling away of the—," I began.

"Yeah," she agreed.

I realized I was having another conversation in the library with a girl. And I wasn't blushing. I guess it was because I started talking to Brynn without planning to talk to her. Now I really was beginning to understand why Joe kept wandering off with her.

"You haven't seen Joe around, have you?" I asked.

"Not for a while," she said. And I was hit with how cute she was. I knew she was cute. I'd noticed it before. But it suddenly hit me—like a sucker punch. That's when I felt the Blush.

"I'll, uh, see you later." I rushed out of the room and continued looking for Joe.

No Joe on the third floor.

No Joe on the second floor.

No Joe on the first floor.

I reached the basement and looked through the tiny window in the sauna door. My pulse started to race—

*Joe.*

He was sprawled out on the wooden planks. Motionless. Bobby and James lay beside him.

I grabbed the door—yanked it. Locked. No, jammed.

*How long have they been in there?* I thought as I scanned the door, trying to figure out the problem. *Did they pass out, or are they—*

"No!" I burst out. "It's not too late." I wasn't going to let it be too late.

There was a workshop on the basement level. I'd seen it the night we checked out the bowling alley.

I jerked around and tore out of there. Through the locker room. Through the gym. Down the hall. *Right or left? Right or left?*

This place was too huge!

I went left, praying that was the way to the work-shop. Yes! I charged inside. I knew exactly what I needed. I ran my eyes over the tools hanging neatly on the wall. There it was.

A chainsaw.

I was back at the sauna door in seconds. I yanked on the safety goggles and the work gloves I'd found. I got the saw going with two quick pulls. Then I attacked the wall. Going at it as far away from where I'd seen the guys as I could.

There was probably a better way to do it. Maybe even a faster way. But this was the first way I thought of.

The chainsaw bucked under my grip as I struggled to carve out a hunk of wall large enough to get a body through. *A person*, I corrected myself. *Not a body. A person.*

"What is going on here?" I heard someone yell from behind me. I thought it was Veronica.

"Three people are passed out in there and the door won't open. That's what's going on," I shouted. I kept on sawing, sweat running down my back, the grip getting hot under my hands.

A jagged rectangle of wood finally fell to the sauna floor. I turned off the chainsaw.

"This is one of the stupidest, most irresponsible things I've ever seen."

I put down the saw and glanced over my shoulder. Yeah, it was Veronica. Ripley, Olivia, and Wilson were clustered behind her.

"We'll have to talk about it later." I leaned through the opening I'd created. I was relieved to see that the chunk of wood hadn't hurt anyone.

And the sound of the chainsaw must have revived Joe, James, and Bobby T. They were huddled as far away from the spot I'd gone in as possible.

"Can you guys walk?" I asked. "Can somebody get them some water?"

"I'll go," Ripley said.

"Getting a little cooler air in here is already helping. The thermostat was jammed too," Joe told me. He helped Bobby T over to the new "door." Together we eased him out of the sauna.

"All I want is an ice-cold shower," he said.

"Cool, not cold," I said. "And first just sit for a while in the air-conditioning."

"Are we going to have to call 911 again?" Veronica asked as James climbed through the hole. His legs were trembling.

"I don't think they have heatstroke. They're still sweating, which is good," I answered. I got Joe out. "You okay?" I asked.

"Kind of nauseous. A headache. It's kind of like when I went on the Screaming Eagle coaster eleven times in a row," Joe said. Ripley handed him a bottle of water.

"Sip it," I ordered. "You guys too," I told James and Bobby T.

I never wanted to live through a day like that again. But I had to watch myself live it over and over. The next day a clip of me and the chainsaw was on a bunch of news shows. I figured Dad had been able to do damage control with Aunt Trudy and Mom. Otherwise they'd already have flown out here and dragged Joe and me home.

All fourteen of us spent the entire day watching anything on TV that mentioned the accident. No one was calling it anything but an accident, even though anyone who had looked at the door or the thermostat knew it wasn't one. I figured Veronica had managed to do some spin when she leaked the tapes.

She'd definitely gotten the door and thermostat out of sight fast. Mitch had practically dismantled the sauna before Joe and I could check it out for evidence.

We were still in the great room late that night—make that a quarter of the great room. Everyone seemed to want to stay close together. There hadn't been any real protests when Veronica had announced that we were losing the use of most of the bathrooms. We'd only have two to share from now on. I bet if she'd tried to pull the plug on the TV, there would have been a riot.

Now we were watching *The Midnight Hour*. No one had gone to bed yet, not even Mary or Hal, and they usually crashed pretty early.

Bobby T kept only half an eye on the plasma. He kept checking the counter on his blog. "I'm getting so many hits," he told us all. "I'm telling you, death sells. Even near death. And I had two near deaths in two days. Plus the death threats that we all got."

He sounded way too happy. Maybe it's because he really needed money, like Olivia said. If he could get the option on his blog renewed and the movie made, he could get out of debt, whether he won the contest or not.

My spine went cold as I pictured my brother, James, and Bobby T passed out in the sauna. Could Bobby T have sabotaged the door and the thermostat? He could have rigged the door to jam when it closed. And he could have rigged the thermostat earlier in the day. Could he be desperate enough to risk his own life to get more hits on his blog?

"I'm trying to decide which clip got more play— Ripley's or Frank's," Mikey said.

<u>Name</u>: Bobby Tibbins

<u>Hometown</u>: Chowchila, California

<u>Physical description</u>: 5'6", 155 lbs., sandy hair currently dyed blue, hazel eyes.

<u>Occupation</u>: High school student/blogger/movie producer.

<u>Background</u>: Skipped a grade in elementary school; housebound for half a year in seventh grade with mononucleosis and started his blog; parents and two sisters have limited interest in the Internet.

<u>Suspicious behavior</u>: Seems happy that he's almost died twice in two days.

<u>Suspected of</u>: Sending death threats to all contestants including himself, staging near deaths for himself.

<u>Possible motive</u>: In deep debt and needs money. Hopes an exciting bunch of blog entries will do it.

"Like we care," James muttered.

"Actually, both were Bobby T clips," Bobby T reminded everyone.

"I did a quick calculation," Rosemary said. "Frank's

clip ran twenty-two percent more often."

"Which is so unfair!" Ripley exclaimed. "I'm the celebrity. I've been in *People* magazine. I was a guest host on *The Scene*."

"You've been in *Star* magazine a lot," Brynn added.

Ripley glared at her. "I was in *Forest of Blood 4*."

"Oh, right. That was you who got killed off right in the beginning," said Mikey.

"If I give you a thousand dollars, will you just shut your mouth?" Ripley screamed at him. She whirled toward Brynn. "You too!"

I was seeing the PR problem now.

Ripley covered her face with her hands. "I'm sorry," she said. "I'm really sorry. I'll leave now."

"Don't go," Brynn said. "So you had a hissy fit. It's okay. You're stressed. We're all stressed."

"I'm stressed!" Kit howled. "I have had no caffeine since yesterday morning."

"That's actually supposed to make you calmer," put in Mary.

"I'm unique, okay?" Kit screeched.

"See?" Brynn said to Ripley. "Kit just had herself a full-on hissy too. It's no big."

"But everyone is going to see mine." Ripley shook her head. "You know they're going to use that on the show. That's the Ripley people want to see—

insane, spoiled Ripley. That five seconds will probably be on every commercial."

She was probably right.

"Aw, poor little rich girl," James snarked.

"Who has a piece of paper?" asked Brynn.

Hal tore a piece off the bottom of his current planet sketch and handed it to her. She wiggled her fingers, and he handed her the pen, too. Brynn curled her left hand around the paper and wrote something down. "Pass it to Rip," she told me.

I made sure to read it without looking like I was reading it as I gave the note to Ripley. It's not a cool thing to do, but Joe and I needed to know everything that was going on in this place. Things were getting too dangerous to miss any clue.

The note said: "I bet Mitch could erase a few minutes of film. Oopsie!"

Ripley smiled when she read what Brynn had written. "Sorry again, everyone. I—"

"Brian's talking about the show in his monologue," Kit cried.

Everyone's attention snapped back to the TV. "Nobody knows what this new show's about," Brian, host of *The Midnight Hour*, was saying. "But I think it's finally happened. We're going to get to watch an actual death, live on TV. And as a bonus, it's going to be the death of an American teen. And they all deserve it, don't they? It's not as if they're going to take care of us in our old age. Selfish monsters."

Rosemary stood up.

"You going to bed?" Kit asked her.

Rosemary didn't answer. She walked over to the intercom by the door and pressed the talk button. "Veronica, I want the fifty thousand dollars. I want to leave here tonight."

"Interesting. That's not the way I thought it would go," Veronica immediately answered through the com. "I'll make out the check. You go pack up your things."

"Rosemary, no!" Mikey exclaimed. "Don't leave."

"He's right." Rosemary jerked her head toward the plasma, where Brian was still doing his monologue. "Someone is going to die here. The attempts are coming very close together. Four out of the fourteen of us have already been affected." She sucked in a deep breath. "That isn't a good percentage."

"Rosemary—," Wilson began.

James interrupted him. "She wants to go, she should go. Don't you understand the concept of competition? Less people, better chance of winning."

"Rosemary, at least think about it a little more," said Wilson.

"It's all I have been thinking about," she answered. "I want to win. I want a million dollars. But I want to stay alive more. And leaving Deprivation House now is the best way to do that."

## 160 Pounds of Rage

"All right, everyone. Are you ready to hear about your next competition?" Veronica asked. She stood in front of the fountain, dressed in a peach outfit. She had a toy poodle as an accessory. It was dyed to match her suit.

There were mumbles and grunts in response.

"Where's the enthusiasm?" Veronica exclaimed. The poodle yipped. "You're competing to win a million dollars, and all I see is sluggishness and lack of ambition."

"I'm ready! Yeah!" James gave a fist pump. "I'm gonna stomp on the slugs! Yeah!"

Veronica closed her eyes briefly. "Thank you, James. Now, how many of you have ever had a pet?"

The majority of hands went up. Rosemary would have had the exact percentage calculated in a second.

"And how many of you swore that you'd take care of the pet in every way, but ended up letting Mommy or the maid do it?" Veronica asked.

Less hands, but still quite a few.

"Well, at Deprivation House, as you're finding out, you do your own chores," she said. "Today you'll be washing the dog. With these." She nodded to Mitch. He moved from person to person, passing out toothbrushes. "And only these. You're not allowed to use your fingers to scrub the beasties."

"Whew, Mitch, you smell foul, my man," Kit said as she got her toothbrush. "It's a preview of what we have to deal with, isn't it?"

"'Fraid so," answered Mitch.

"What if one of us has a small dog phobia?" Mikey asked. "Not a phobia of small dogs. A small fear of dogs."

Veronica smiled at him. "Then one of us won't have much of a chance of winning."

"That's right," James said smugly.

There were times I wished James was the perp, just so I could help put him away. But ATAC agents are trained to keep their emotions out of their missions, so I ignored those wishes.

"You'll find the dogs out behind the tennis

courts. Each dog's collar has one of your names on it. Whoever gets his or her dog cleanest in an hour wins." She made shooing motions with her hands.

We all raced to the dogs. They were tied with long leashes to hitching posts that had been positioned all over the field. I ran to the closest "empty" pup—a floppy-eared hound dog. A stinky, floppy-eared hound dog. I didn't know what he'd been rolling in and I didn't want to know. Whatever it was seemed to involve chunks. I checked his collar. "This one's yours, Wilson," I called.

Maybe that wasn't the best strategy. I was helping the competition. But Frank won't let me keep the money anyway. . . .

"Joe, this guy's yours!" I heard Ripley yell. She pointed to an extremely large—I was thinking 160 pounds large—extremely hairy Newfoundland. Oh, well. At least Newfies were known for their great temperament.

"You won't mind getting scrubbed with a toothbrush, will you, boy?" I asked when I reached him. I was glad to see that a hose, shampoo, and towel were sitting in a bucket next to the dog.

I studied Hairy—I had to call him something, and I thought Putrid might get us off on the wrong foot. What was the best way to approach this? I wondered if I should use the towel to get off at least the top layer of . . . I really didn't want to look too close.

No, I decided. There was only one towel. I'd have to burn it if I touched Hairy with it right now, and then I wouldn't have anything to dry him off with later. "Here's the plan," I told him. "First we rinse."

I turned on the hose and started spraying Hairy down. Some of the chunks ran off his fur. A lot stayed stuck to him.

Hairy turned his head toward me and gave a low growl.

"What's the problem?" I asked him, still spraying him. "You guys are supposed to love water. Pull drowning sailors out of the ocean and all that. Are you telling me this is bothering you?"

Hairy gave me a don't-play-me stare. When his fur was saturated with water, which took awhile, because probably twenty of those 160 pounds had to be hair, I turned off the hose. "Okay, we're done with that. Now I'm going to give you a nice toothbrush massage. All the better dogs are having them. Look around, you'll see."

I pointed to Ripley and an Afghan hound. Hairy didn't seem impressed. "Okay, it was a stupid thing to say," I told him as I crouched down next to him. I popped the top of the soap and put dabs of it all the way down his back.

His hackles came up in rough ridges, and he growled again. This time his upper lip curled high, showing me a mouthful of serious teeth.

"This is an unfair thing to do to you dogs," I said calmly and softly, holding my body still. "We agreed to come here. We might win a million, not that we can keep it, because of our brother. But you guys, what are you getting? I'd be mad too."

Hairy's hackles didn't go down. His lip stayed pulled back. He had a continuous growl going now, barely audible, from deep in his throat. This dog wasn't just a dog who didn't want a bath. This wasn't a dog who was a little annoyed.

This was a dog who was thinking about attacking. "I'm going to stand up very slowly and go away now," I told Hairy. I straightened up from my crouch, careful not to look directly at the dog. Eye contact is considered an act of aggression to canines, and I definitely didn't want Hairy to think I was getting aggressive.

As I started to back away, Hairy started to bark. Loud and fast.

I took another step. Hairy lunged. And he had just enough leash to reach me. He brought me down. Hard.

*Go fetal*, I told myself. I covered my head with my arms and curled my legs to my chest. Hairy stood over me, barking. Half my body was under his.

I heard footsteps running toward me. Hairy's barking turned frantic.

"Stay back," I heard Frank call out. "We're making him more aggressive."

I could feel Hairy's hot breath on my head. He was really panting hard. *They're going to figure out what to do,* I told myself. *Just stay still.*

"Joe," Ripley called. "I'm moving toward you on the left. I'm not going to get too close. I don't want to freak out your friend. I'm only going to get close enough to roll some pepper spray into your left hand."

I slid one arm away from my head, feeling like a turtle without the protection of its shell. Slowly I stretched my hand out.

Hairy switched into that low, low growl again. I didn't look at him. I didn't want to risk eye contact. But I figured he was giving Ripley a warning.

"I can't risk getting any nearer. I'm going to roll it now. One, two, three," Ripley said.

I flexed my fingers, and a second later I felt a small, cool canister hit them. I cracked my eyes open, adjusted the pepper spray so it was aimed at Hairy—then pushed the button.

The dog scrambled away with a whimper. I leaped to my feet and got myself well out of the range of

Hairy's long leash. I realized I had Ripley's pepper spray in a death grip. "Thanks." I walked over and handed it back. "So, do you routinely carry this stuff?"

"I use it when the paparazzi get in my face," she answered as Frank, Brynn, and Mikey joined us. Ripley shook her head. "No, I *used* to use it when the paparazzi got in my face. Now I'll let them take pictures whenever. I've got nothing to hide. I'm nice twenty-four/seven. Almost."

"At least you'll have more clips than I do now," Frank told her. "You're a hero again."

We both watched for her reaction. "Hey, I guess I am," she said. "We'll have to check me out on TV."

"You didn't get bitten or anything, did you?" Brynn asked.

Ripley slapped her forehead. "I should have asked that."

"My long-lost brother should have asked that," I said.

"I didn't see any blood," Frank told me.

Suddenly I realized everyone else was back to working on their dogs. "The contest is still on. Veronica didn't call a time out or anything," I told them. "Come on. I want to see those toothbrushes flying. You still have a chance to win."

"You're sure?" Mikey asked.

"Go!" I ordered. He and Ripley took off. Brynn and Frank didn't move. "I'm fine," I told them. "Go." They went.

I looked over at Hairy. Poor guy. He had his tail down and was vomiting into the grass.

A woman with a long gray braid hurried over to him. "Wait," I called. "He's not stable."

She veered away from Hairy and walked over to me. "Are you the boy who was working with Captain?" The woman gestured toward Hairy.

"Yeah, I was," I answered.

"I'm his trainer. I should have been here today. I let a handler bring him. It sounded like a basic job, and I had to—" She stopped. "That's not important. What happened exactly? Captain's never been aggressive with anyone. I let my two-year-old granddaughter ride him around like a pony."

I took another look at Hairy—Captain. He was lying down with his head resting on his front paws. Right now he didn't look like he could hurt a squeaky toy.

"I don't know what they did to the dogs before they got here to get them so dirty," I answered. "But what I did to Captain was start to give him a bath. I got him wet with the hose, and—"

"He loves that. He loves getting wet," Captain's trainer interrupted. "If he can't find anything better, he'll stick his paws in his water dish."

"I put a little shampoo on his back. Not near his eyes or anything," I explained. "Then he was growling and snarling and barking, so I decided to back away slowly. I only got a few steps, and he was on me."

"I don't understand," Captain's trainer said. "I really don't. My poor baby."

"Sorry I had to pepper spray him." I really was. He sounded like a great dog.

"A dog as big and strong as Captain would have been impossible for you to fight off. It's okay," she answered. "I'm going to take him home now. I'll get him all fixed up."

I watched her walk Captain off the field. He stuck right to her heel. He didn't bark once, not at a single person or dog. Weird.

I decided to do a little investigation. I headed over to the scene of the crime. Towel. Shampoo. Hitching post. Toothbrush. Chunks of whatever. Puke.

Actually, puke can be a good source of info. It can help you determine time of death, for example. Of course, it's not a fun source of info to examine.

I picked up the towel and used one end to spread the vomit out. One weird thing I noticed was a couple of seeds. They were kind of kidney shaped. Unless Captain ate some super-crunchy-granola dog chow, I didn't think seeds would be in his puke.

"You're studying vomit? You always get to do the fun stuff," Frank said as he crouched down next to me.

"Don't you have to wash a dog?" I asked.

"I got a dachshund. I'm done," he said.

"What do you think of those seeds?" I pointed one out to him.

Frank picked it up and crushed it between his fingers. Then he raised his hand to his nose and took a deep breath. "Smell," he told me. I leaned away from him. "Just do it."

I took a sniff. "Foul," I muttered.

"Right. Remember the day we went over poisons at ATAC training?" Frank said. "Foul odor was one of the main characteristics of jimsonweed."

I automatically began reciting parts of the rhyme our instructor had taught us to help us learn the effects of the plant. "Mad as a hatter, dry as a bone, red as a beet."

"It would be hard to tell if a dog was red as a beet." Frank threw the crushed seed onto the grass. "But mad as a hatter?"

"I talked to his trainer, and she said he'd never acted that way before," I said. "And the dry as a bone—I noticed Captain wasn't slobbering. I thought it was strange, because I think of Newfies as big, slobbery dogs. Dogs who should practically wear bibs."

"I'm glad he vomited this up. He should be okay with it out of his system," Frank said. "We should have his trainer get him checked out by a vet to be sure."

I nodded. "So since I've had two attempts on my life, how does that change the percentages?" I asked. "It's still four out of fourteen of us who have done the near-death thing. But I don't think that really reflects the situation."

"All I know is, things worked out well for two of our suspects this afternoon," Frank told me.

"Ripley got to be a hero again. She's already expecting TV time. Who else?" I asked.

"I'm sure Bobby T will find a way to make your near death almost as exciting for his readers as one of his own," Frank answered.

"Joe, you've got to check your e-mail," Bobby T said. He gave me a shake.

"What? Do I have fan mail from your bloggers?" I sat up and realized I'd fallen asleep on one of the couches in the great room. "You didn't give out my e-mail address, did you?" I looked around. "What time is it?"

"It's three. Come on, check your mail," Bobby T urged. "I didn't wake everybody else up yet."

Yet?

Bobby T thrust his laptop into my hands. "Why are you awake now?" I asked softly.

"I was up working on my blog. I was about to go to bed, but I figured I'd check e-mail first. Joe, just do it, okay?" Bobby T's voice cracked on the last word. He was really upset. I hadn't realized it faster because I'd been half asleep.

"Sure." I logged onto my server and pulled up my new e-mail.

"That one." Bobby T tapped the screen. "The one with no 'from' address."

I clicked it.

A video launched, even though I hadn't clicked on a file. A skeletal hand holding a shovel began to dig a grave. The hand and the shovel and the ground were all made of construction paper. They didn't look real or anything. But the *shoop, shoop, shoop* sound of the shovel tearing up the earth still gave me the creeps.

The hand and shovel disappeared. Then the hand reappeared holding a little person. The body was construction paper. But the head was a photograph of a real head. My head.

The hand carefully placed "me" into the grave, then refilled the hole with pieces of brown construction-paper earth.

"That was seriously twisted," I said to Bobby T.

"It's not over. At least mine had a message," he answered.

I looked back at the screen. The bone hand now held a piece of chalk. It began to write.

WHAT WILL YOU DO WITH A MILLION DOLLARS WHEN YOU'RE SIX FEET UNDER, JOE? NEXT COMPETITION, SOMEONE DIES.

FRANK

# 12

# Pranks

"I don't want to describe mine. I'm trying to block it out," Brynn said. She took one bite of her cold cereal, then dropped the spoon in the bowl.

I wouldn't mind blocking my e-mail out. But I didn't think I'd be able to. It involved a shark. And my limbs being taken one by one, until I was just a bobbing head all alone in the middle of the ocean. It had ended with the same last line as Joe's. All of us had gotten that same last line: NEXT COMPETITION, SOMEONE DIES.

"I want to know who did it," James told the group.

"We all do," said Joe.

"No, I want to know now. It has to be one of you," he said. "Who else cares?"

126

"Clearly the e-mails were a prank," Veronica said, doing one of her sudden appearances. "Don't any of you have a sense of humor?"

I was still having trouble getting used to the fact that Veronica knew almost everything that happened in the house.

"I might think it was a prank. Not a funny one, but a prank," Kit answered. "Except that people have been in real danger here. Joe almost got mauled by that dog. The sauna almost fried a few people. And Bobby T had to be taken to the hospital."

"You seem to be making connections between those events," Veronica told her. "I see none."

"You don't? I see a big one. I see contestants almost dying over and over again." Kit's voice got higher and thinner with every word.

"Maybe you would like the forty thousand dollars," Veronica suggested gently.

"That isn't what I was saying," Kit snapped.

"I merely wanted to remind you—and everyone— of your options. I know going without your luxuries can be very difficult. It can make some people very short-tempered," Veronica said.

"You want me to drop it? Fine, I'll drop it." Kit took a big bite of her cold piece of bread and butter.

"I didn't ask any such thing," Veronica protested.

"You know, maybe it's something about the house itself that brings out the dark side of human nature. You're all assuming the events have to do with the contest. But this house has quite an unpleasant history."

"What?" I asked. I wanted to know if she was referring to the Katrina Decter murder.

Veronica sat down at the table and poured herself a glass of water. "I don't know if it's true, but they say there was a case of demon possession in this house about eleven years ago."

Some of the color drained out of Brynn's face. Veronica must have been one of those kids who liked pulling wings off flies, I decided. Why else was she telling a horror story now? Like there was such a thing as demonic possession.

"A young actress lived here back then—," Veronica continued.

"Katrina Decter," interrupted Kit.

Veronica sighed, then went on. "She was married to an up-and-coming director." She looked at Kit as if she was waiting for her to interrupt again. "His name was Phillip Jonell. They were very happy. They had a little girl. Then Katrina began to change."

"I remember where else I've heard of her now," Bobby T said. "She was in and out of rehab a lot, right? One of my friends has this cool website. It has the whole history of celebrity rehab."

Veronica sighed again. "May I continue?" She waited until Bobby T nodded, then went on. "Her little girl knew the truth about the change in her mommy. Anna knew a demon had taken over her mommy's body. Sometimes she could even see the demon's face on top of her mommy's face."

I really hated the way Veronica talked to us like we were kindergartners. Kindergartners who misbehaved a lot.

"She saw the demon especially clearly one night when she was four years old. The night the demon tried to kill her," Veronica said.

"I'm lost," said Ripley. "I thought the little girl testified that her mother tried to kill her father, and that her father killed her mother in self-defense."

"That's what Anna said at the trial. She described in great detail the hideous demon's face and how it attacked her father," Veronica agreed. "But Phillip testified that Katrina went after Anna first."

Huh. So the little girl said the mother had attacked the father, and that's why the father had killed her. But the father had said that the mother had tried to murder the little girl, so he had killed the mother to save the little girl.

There was definitely a mystery to be solved

there. But Katrina Decter was already dead. This case involved people we were trying to keep alive. It had priority.

"Story time is over." Veronica stood up. "Today we'll be taking away cable television. We'll also be replacing the plasmas with less luxurious TV sets. I bet some of you didn't even know that television could be shown in black-and-white. And you will only be allowed to watch television at all between the hours of eight and ten p.m."

She started for the door, then turned back to face us all. "Oh, and meet me in the screening room in half an hour, please. It will be unsealed for the occasion." She waited.

"What occasion?" Mary asked.

"It's a sad one," Veronica said. "I'm afraid it's time for me to send one of you home. Can you believe a week has flown by already?"

I don't think the plush seats of the screening room were comfortable for anyone as we waited for Veronica to appear and give us the verdict. Joe and I had to stay in the house until we wrapped the mission. But it wasn't as if ATAC could pull strings with Veronica. She didn't know we were undercover. No one on the show did.

It's better that way. Safer. You never know going

into a mission who is involved in the crime you're investigating.

The lights dimmed. The velvet curtain in front of the screen swished open. "What's this about?" Joe asked from the row behind me. I shrugged in reply.

Low alt-rock started up as clips from the house began to play. The film was of different quality, depending on whether it was from the handhelds or the cameras mounted in the rooms.

Someone had gotten a close-up of Joe whimpering as he watched the pool getting drained. I laughed. He looked so pouty. Then I remembered. The person getting booted was the one who hadn't been able to deal with losing the luxuries. Whimpering over the pool wasn't exactly dealing.

There was a shot of Ripley wrinkling her nose as she laid frozen Tater Tots on a baking sheet. And shots of almost all of us half gagging on the meal where James had been head cook.

A camera had caught an iPod-less Brynn with her pinkies in her ears. She was humming. Loudly.

I got to see the appetizing sight of myself spitting a big mouthful of James's disgusting dinner into my napkin.

*No one made it through the week without some kind of not-dealing behavior*, I realized as the film went on.

Then came about twenty quick shots of Kit saying the word "coffee." Not just saying it, actually. Screaming it. Shrieking it. Whining it. Whimpering it. Crying it. Howling it. Whispering it. Laughing it. Snarling it.

The short movie ended with Kit declaring, "I can't live without coffee!"

As the lights came back up, Veronica strolled to the front of the room. "Eye opening, wasn't it? And you all thought you would have no problem giving up a few little items."

I glanced over at Kit. About half the people in the room were glancing over at Kit.

"Still, I think there was one *performance* that really stood out. I'm sure none of you will be surprised to hear what I'm about to say." She took a deep breath and smiled. "Kit Elroy, you have been deprived of the chance to win one million dollars!"

Veronica announced it with as much enthusiasm as if Kit had won the million. The woman was a seriously twisted human being.

Kit stood up. "It's been great getting to know—"

"No speeches," Veronica cut her off. "You aren't accepting an Oscar. Go upstairs and pack your things. You need to leave immediately."

"Okay. Bye." Kit rushed out fast, but I thought I saw tears streaking her face.

"The rest of us have to take care of a little business," Veronica said calmly, not giving us a chance to say a word. "James, you won the dog-washing competition. Did you decide what luxury you want taken away next?"

"Yep. Junk food," he announced.

He was that kind of guy. He was all about finding his competitors' weak spots. He knew Mikey really wanted to keep junk food, so he took it away.

"Your body will thank me," James added to Mikey. "If you last long enough in here, you'll drop that gut."

Yeah. He was all about finding the weak spots.

"The only other thing I have to say is, get some rest. We're having a competition tomorrow," Veronica told us.

I bet everyone in the room was wondering the same thing. Was someone really going to die at the competition?

## That's Extreme

"**W**e have to find out what the competition for tomorrow is going to be," Frank told me once we were in the camera-free storage closet.

"Definitely. We have to do a full safety check on all the equipment," I agreed. "The problem is, the info on the competition has to be in—"

"Veronica's quarters," Frank finished for me. "And she never lets anyone up there. We're not allowed anywhere on the third floor."

"And there are cameras everywhere." Like anyone in the house needed reminding of that.

"Sounds like the perfect time to try out the latest ATAC technology," Frank suggested. "They sent over that anticamera device about a month ago, remember?"

"You brought it?" I asked.

"Yep."

"It's kind of conspicuous," I said. It was cool, though. See, digital cameras—which the ones mounted around the house were—put out a beam of light. Either visible or invisible. The anticamera device can sense these beams. And when they do, they shoot back an infrared laser into the camera lens, and—camera neutralized.

"It's bulky, though. We're going to look suspicious walking around with it," I told Frank.

"I can disguise it as a laptop. Bobby T wanders around with his open all the time. And James is always playing some game on his," said Frank.

"I was thinking about both those guys. And Hal," I said. "I was thinking they all possibly have the computer savvy to put together the e-mails everyone got. James is really into hacking his games—so he can win faster. Hal is planning to design a video game after he designs his planet. And Bobby T, well, is Bobby T."

"That's definitely something we should consider. But those three aren't necessarily the only ones with the know-how to create the e-mails," Frank replied. "The problem is, we still don't know the suspects that well. There are too many of them."

"And people keep trying to kill us. Well, me," I said.

"Yeah, that's a problem too." Frank rubbed his face with his fingers. "Okay, let's prioritize. There's a competition tomorrow. We've been warned—threatened—that someone's going to die then."

"I'd say finding out the competition plans is top of the list," I said. "So we use the anticamera device to deal with the surveillance situation. And, by the way, anticamera device—could ATAC come up with a more boring name, you think?"

"I just care that it works," Frank answered. "That's only step one. We're also going to need Veronica out of her quarters for a while."

"She usually stays in her lair the whole night." I thought for a minute. "She did come down pretty fast when Rosemary decided to leave. And she didn't go back upstairs until she'd gotten Rosemary off to the airport."

"We can't make somebody drop out," Frank said. "Can we?"

"They'd get forty thousand. And a really good chance not to die young," I reminded him. "Not that we're going to let anyone die, but still."

"Good point. So who do we deprive of the chance to be a millionaire?" Frank asked.

"I wish we could give James the boot, but no way

could we convince him to leave," I said. "Mikey? He really isn't happy about losing his junk food. He might end up getting sent home next week anyway."

"Yeah, but I get the feeling he'll be okay. I don't think he'll lose it the way Kit did over the coffee," Frank reasoned. "Maybe Wilson?"

"But he's finally getting a girlfriend thing going," I protested. "We can't pull him and Olivia apart."

"Olivia's only talking to him so much because she's considering him as an alliance member," said Frank.

"He doesn't seem to have another possible love connection on the back burner." I thought about it. "Let's give him the scoop on Olivia and tell him we'll get Bobby T to do a blog entry about him that will get lots of girls interested in him. And remind him that forty thousand is a lot of lettuce."

I felt a little slimy about it, but Wilson actually sounded pretty relieved when he got on the intercom early that evening and told Veronica he wanted his check and a cab to the airport. Dropouts didn't get limos.

Frank and I got the anticamera device—I was going to work on that name myself—powered up. As soon as we spotted Veronica coming down the stairs to the third floor, we made our move.

Her door was locked, of course. But we covered locked doors the first day of ATAC training. I handled it this time. I pulled out my lock pick. A few twists, a pull, and we were in.

I couldn't imagine Veronica being that comfortable in these rooms. They were too . . . cozy. More old-fashioned than the stuff downstairs.

"There's her computer. Let's hope she didn't take the time to log off." I checked. "She did."

"Of course she did. Doesn't she seem like someone who would?" Frank asked.

"Someone like you?" I immediately held up my hands in surrender. "I take it back. She may have a few, uh, orderly qualities. If she wore jeans, she'd probably iron them. I mean, her shoes always match her dress—an exact match. But you, my brother, are a nice, good person. She's a person who'd . . . give out sugarless gum on Halloween and laugh."

"If she is *orderly*, that means it's going to take awhile to figure out her password. I follow all the advice on how to make them tough to crack." Frank grinned. "But a truly orderly person would print out a hard copy of something as important as competition plans."

"I'll check the baseboards and the—"

"I doubt they'll be hidden. Her quarters are really

secure. Think what we had to do to get in here," Frank said.

"But she took the time to log off the computer," I pointed out.

"That's different. It's a habit." Frank opened the top desk drawer and found the hard copy of the plans. Show-off.

I tilted my head back and cracked my neck.

He flipped through the pages. "I've got enough of it that we'll know where we need to go to do a safety check," he said as he returned the plans to the desk drawer.

"I noticed that one of the ceiling beams is crooked," I told him. "How'd that happen in the perfect villa?"

"I don't know. I do know we need to get out of here," Frank answered.

"Look at it for one second. It's . . . not right." My Spidey sense was twanging.

Frank looked up. "Huh. Yeah. With the quality of work on this place, I don't get how that happened. It's only a little off, but still."

I checked out the other ceiling beams in the room. "I don't think it's actually weight-bearing," I said.

"It definitely wouldn't have to be with the way the ceiling is constructed," Frank agreed. "Come on. Let's go."

"I want to see something. I read something once about fake beams used as hiding places. People hollow them out and put stuff in them. I wonder if that could be the deal here." I looked around for something to climb on that would give me a better look. Why did the ceilings in this place have to be so high?

"Don't even think about it, Joe," Frank warned as I started toward a massive, freestanding closet thing. A wardrobe, they'd call it in England.

"We're detectives. We can't pass this by. It'll only take a second," I said in a rush. "And I'm not leaving until I look, so give me a boost."

Frank came over and made a stirrup out of his hands. I put one foot in and he launched me up. Good thing the wardrobe was so heavy, or I'd have knocked it over. I shoved myself to my feet and sidestepped over to the beam. I probed it gently. I definitely didn't want to bring it down if it turned out to be moveable.

A panel in the bottom of the beam slid free—and fat stacks of money plopped down on the floor. I was shocked, and I was the one who thought the beam might have been used as a hiding place.

Frank stared at the cash. "There's a ton of money here," he said.

"Now what?"

"I don't get how this fits in with the case so far. But it's got to be important." Frank started gathering up the stacks and tossing them to me. "Let's put it back for now. We don't want anyone to know the money has been discovered."

"I couldn't maybe keep one stack?" I asked as I slid the panel back in place. "I'm sure no one would notice. I doubt they count it every night."

Frank ignored me. I wonder if there is a *Bonehead's Guide for Developing a Sense of Humor.*

We kept the anticamera on even when we'd made it out of the house, flashlights in hand. We didn't know exactly what the surveillance situation was outdoors. There were definitely some cameras positioned around the pool, but it would take hundreds of them to observe all the land that was part of the villa property.

"The big thing tomorrow is a lawn mower race. We're each going to mow sections of that field where we did the dog wash," Frank explained. "But there's going to be an obstacle course first. We'll have to make it through to get to the mowers. The fastest people will get the best ones."

We began working our way around the course, checking everything. Ropes. Inner tubes. A trampoline. A zip line. Crawling tubes. A balance beam. An inflatable wall.

"I can see how somebody might get hurt trying to make it through the obstacles too fast. But I didn't see any signs of sabotage," I said when we reached the end.

"Me either. All we have left to go over are the mowers. I think if we don't find anything, we should make another pass in the morning." Frank's face was troubled. "I think whoever sent the e-mail was serious. That doesn't mean they'll actually kill anybody. But they'll do something."

"We should do a check as close to go time as we can," I agreed. We started across the field to the row of mowers at the far end. "It will probably have to be before breakfast. It's going to be hard to get away after that. We have the cameras under control, but we can't keep nine other people—plus maybe Veronica and some PAs—from asking questions about where we're going."

Frank nodded. "Let's get started on these. You might need a tetanus shot if you touch that one, but that's probably it." He pointed toward a rusted-out push mower.

"Oh, man, this is the one I wanted Dad to get. It has some muscle. Twenty-six horsepower," I said. I ran my hand over the garden tractor's deep red paint job.

"Our lawn doesn't need twenty-six horsepower,"

Frank replied. "It only needs the power of the Hardy boys. Isn't that what Dad said when you asked him to buy it?"

"Pretty much." I was going to get a look at the engine. Not because I wanted to. I had to. For the mission.

"Frank, come over here," I said.

"No time. I'm checking this one," he told me.

"Forget it! I found what we're looking for." My stomach twisted into a knot as I thought about what could have happened. "There's a bomb wired to the ignition."

Frank dashed over. "Let's get it out of there." He leaned over the engine and studied the bomb's connection to the mower. "I think—"

He stopped abruptly as a beam of bright white light slashed across his face. I squinted as it cut across mine.

"Come away from there immediately," a familiar voice ordered. Veronica.

"We found a—," I began to explain.

"I have no interest in hearing anything cheaters have to say," Veronica told us as we walked over to her. "Why do you think you deserve an early look at what the competition entails? It's completely unfair. You're both out."

She raised a walkie-talkie to her mouth. "Mitch,

I found them on the field. I want you to come and take them to your quarters."

"Veronica, it's very important—," Frank started.

Mitch arrived. "Take these two to your quarters. Stay with them. Don't let them out of your sight. They aren't slinking home until tomorrow. I want footage." Veronica turned on her heel and left the three of us standing there.

Frank turned to Mitch. "She wouldn't listen to us. You need to. There's a bomb in that mower."

Mitch immediately went over and looked. He let out a long, low whistle. "Things are getting way too intense around this place. I just wanted to make a little money."

"You're going to tell her, right?" I asked.

"Definitely. Then I'm going to stay far away while somebody who knows how to deal with those things gets that bomb out of there," he answered. "But look, I've got to take you over to my place. Veronica is going to flip if I don't. Then nobody will be able to talk to her."

He led the way to a little guest cottage out of sight of the main house. "Pretty sweet, huh?" he said. "There are a few of these places scattered around, and I got assigned one."

Mitch unlocked the door and ushered us inside. "I'm not going to lock you in or anything. But stay put until Veronica recovers and I talk to her. Make yourselves at home. I have some drinks in the fridge. There are some glasses in the cupboard. To living through it, right?" He gave us a half salute and left.

I sank down on the blue-and-white-striped sofa. Frank took the armchair across from me. "I can't believe she wouldn't listen."

"She practically stuck her fingers in her ears. She's a nut job," I agreed. "At least Mitch is cool." I shoved myself to my feet. "I think I am going to get something to drink. You want one?"

"Yeah. Thanks," Frank said.

I found the kitchen, grabbed some sodas, decided to skip the glasses, and headed back to the living room. Frank didn't even complain that I was making him drink out of the can. That's how wiped he was.

I raised my can toward him. "To living through—"

"Whatever it is," Frank joined in, finishing our toast. Suddenly he sat straight up. "We came up with that our first day."

"Yeah."

"Joe, that was before Mitch started working on the show," Frank said.

"Maybe he saw some film from that day," I suggested. "That's probably part of his job, searching through it for usable stuff."

"But they didn't get any outdoor footage the first day. There was some technical mess-up," Frank reminded me.

"Right. That PA said something to Veronica about it, and Veronica practically turned her into an ice sculpture." I took a slug of soda, my mind whirling. "That means Mitch was there the night before Leo died. He was there the night before there was any way he could have known there was a job opening."

"Unless he knew he was going to kill Leo," Frank said.

"For a job?" I shook my head. "That's extreme."

"Maybe that wasn't the motive. Maybe he didn't kill Leo. All I know is that I don't want to sit around waiting for him to come back." Frank stood up.

"I'm with you, my brother." I drained my soda and headed out the door.

The night was dark, but everything went darker.

Everything went black as pain exploded in the back of my head.

And I was falling. . . .

## Mad as a Hatter

All I knew at first was that I definitely wasn't at home. Then I realized I shouldn't be at home. Then I realized I wasn't in my bunk bed in the villa. And then I basically remembered everything and realized I was lying on the floor of what I thought was Mitch's place. I was tied back-to-back with somebody I assumed was Joe, and as I blinked, I realized daylight was coming in through the window. Whoa, it was already morning? We'd been out all night?

Maybe it had something to do with the fuzzy feeling in my head—my eyes scanned the room, and sure enough, landed on a syringe in the corner.

Mitch must have pumped us with sedatives after

knocking us out, to keep us out of play for all this time.

A pair of boots clomped by. "You're awake," Mitch said. "Sorry I had to knock you guys out. But I told you to stay in the cabin, and less than five minutes later, you come sneaking out. You didn't give me a choice. You've seen how Veronica is."

*Okay, so Mitch didn't hear us talking about him,* I thought. That was something. We had a little bit of an edge as long as he didn't know we were suspicious of him. It wasn't much of an edge, though— since we were tied up on the floor.

"Yeah, Veronica." I cleared my throat. "We didn't want to deal with her. Weren't trying to get you in trouble."

"Well, you would have," Mitch shot back.

As he rattled off a list of what Veronica would have done to him if we'd managed to escape, Joe started up a silent conversation with me. Tapping out a Morse code message against my side. It took awhile for him to dot-and-dash out what he had to say: "Big mirror near me."

I remembered a big mirror in Mitch's living room. "So?" I Morsed back.

"Roll hard. My go," Joe Morsed. Out loud, he apologized to Mitch.

I didn't know what Joe's message meant exactly.

But it involved rolling on Joe's signal. Rolling toward the mirror, I was pretty sure.

Joe coughed loudly. "Something reeks over here," he said. "It's foul." He gave me a nudge.

"Let's not talk," said Mitch. "I'll just turn the TV on while we wait for Veronica to get here. She wants to get some footage of you with the other kids. Their faces when they hear you were cheating and all that."

I thought I knew where Joe had been going with the "foul" comment. I remembered Kit teasing Mitch about smelling foul not too long before the dog-washing contest. Joe was thinking Mitch had something to do with giving the bad-smelling jimsonweed to Captain.

"It does smell nasty. Maybe you aren't getting a whiff up there, but it's like jimsonweed," I said as Mitch started flipping channels.

Bringing up the jimsonweed was a risk. Right now, Mitch didn't realize we were suspicious of him. But mentioning the jimson could tip him off. Or he might just think—and this is what we were hoping—that we honestly just smelled the jimson in his place and didn't have any idea jimsonweed had been fed to the dog.

"It grows around here. I bet you tracked some in," Joe said. "You've got to let us up."

"Uh, I don't think so," Mitch told him.

"You don't get it," Joe went on. "Most people think that stuff is only poison if you eat it. But if it releases spores in an enclosed space, it can kill you too. Just more slowly."

"We have our noses right in it. We have to with the way it smells down here," I added.

"Do you know the symptoms, Frank?" Joe asked.

I went into the rhyme. "Mad as a hatter, red as a beet, dry as a bone, the heart runs alone."

"I'm definitely dry. It's like I have no saliva in my mouth," Joe said. "And heart runs alone—that's like fast heartbeat, right?"

"Yeah. I can feel mine going right now."

I thought it was possible, at least a little possible, that Mitch might be feeling some of those symptoms right now. Not because he was somehow getting jimsonweed poisoning through the air. That wasn't possible.

But dry mouth, red face, accelerated heartbeat—those were all also symptoms of anxiety. And Mitch had a couple of things to be anxious about. He might be thinking he could have maybe brought a little jimsonweed into the house accidentally. That might be making him nervous. Or he might be remembering how he primed the Newfie to attack Joe. That would do it too. Maybe he was thinking about what he did to Leo—if Joe and I were right about that. Yeah, he had a few reasons to be a little twitchy.

Besides, if you talk about symptoms, some people start to feel them. "I can't see if my face is red," Joe said. "Mitch, dude, just mop the floor or something. Seriously, I don't want to be sucking jimson into my body."

"Veronica isn't going to be happy if we're dead when she comes out here," I added.

I heard Mitch take a step toward us. Or maybe toward the mirror. *Yeah, Mitch, you want to look in the mirror. You want to see if your face is red. You don't want to end up poisoned, do you?* I thought.

More footsteps. Joe gave me a jab. Mitch had to be getting close to the mirror. It was almost time to roll.

Joe tapped me on the side. One. Two. Three. The next one was it—

And go.

I rolled as hard as I could. I didn't worry about smashing Joe. All I wanted was for the Joe-Frank combo to hit Mitch as hard as it could.

Over and over and *crunch*.

Mitch and the mirror collided. I don't know how hard the impact was, but it had happened. A shard of the glass had fallen near enough that my fingers could just reach it. I used it to start sawing on whatever Mitch had used to tie us. I could feel warm blood dripping down my hand. Didn't matter.

The ties loosened a little. I thought Joe managed to wriggle an arm free. Must have, because I heard Mitch give a grunt of pain.

Now that Joe's arm was out, the ties were even looser. I got an arm free. Getting the next one loose was easy. Joe and I both attacked the ties now. I shot a glance at Mitch. In the broken mirror, I could see that blood was running down his forehead. And he was crouched low. Like maybe Joe had managed to get a shot in behind his knee.

He definitely wasn't down for the count. He turned to face us as we made it to our feet.

I caught a glimpse of motion out the window. A figure bouncing up and down on a trampoline in the distance. The others had started running the obstacle course.

Mitch saw where I was looking. "Too late," he said.

"Not hardly." Joe arched back and slammed his fist into Mitch's jaw. KO. "You go," he told me. "I'll clean up the mess in here." He reached for the restraints.

That's all I needed to hear. I took off, pain ricocheting through my numb legs. I ignored it.

I had one thing to focus on right now—getting to the garden tractor before anyone turned the ignition key and set off the bomb.

 **JOE**

I finished tying Mitch up, my brain clicking away. I couldn't figure out a motive for Mitch killing Leo and trying to kill the contestants.

He murdered Leo to get his job—okay. Seemed like a weak motive, but okay. But why keep killing after he got the job?

What possible motive could he have for wanting us contestants dead? It's not like if he killed everybody off, he'd get the million dollars. So it wasn't about money.

Or wait. Was it? I flashed on the money in Veronica's ceiling beam. Had Mitch hidden it upstairs—before everyone from the show moved in, maybe? Then he couldn't get it back, because Veronica wouldn't let anyone onto her floor and there were cameras all over.

It kind of made sense. Mitch killed Leo to get the job. But having the job wasn't enough. It didn't get him the access he needed.

What he needed was everybody out of the house. The threats and dangerous stuff—that had been Mitch trying to get the show shut down. He'd

planned to step it up to murder of a show partici-
pant today. He probably figured that would put the
end to everything.

I stared down at Mitch. His eyelids began to flut-
ter. He was coming to.

"You said to make myself at home before. So I'm
going to ransack the place looking for evidence," I
told him.

Mitch glared up at me. He was really hating me
right now.

I was fine with that.

I headed for the computer first. You can get a lot
of evidence off a computer. It took me about three
seconds to find out that my buddy Mitch had been
researching poisonous plants—including jimsonweed.

He'd also been reading articles about a bank robbery that had taken place about a year ago. About
twenty-five thousand dollars had been stolen.

That got me wondering what Mitch's record
might be like. I spotted a felt-tip pen near the mouse
pad. I grabbed it and hurried back over to Mitch.

I inked up his fingers, then transferred his prints
onto a piece of white paper.

"Those aren't going to tell you anything," he said.
"I'm too smart to leave prints."

I used Mitch's computer to scan the prints and

send them to Vijay. I got his response in less than a minute. "You weren't too smart to go to prison for assault."

Mitch laughed. "That was nothing."

I thought again of the money hidden in the hollowed-out beam in Veronica's quarters. "Yeah, it didn't earn you twenty-five thou like your bank job, did it?" I asked.

Mitch's eyes widened.

"Not that you got to spend much of it. Since you got locked up for that little nothing assault thing," I added.

## FRANK

I hauled myself up an enormous spiderweb of rope strung between two trees. I hadn't been taking the obstacles. I wasn't a contestant. But I had to scale the web. It was the shortest way to get past it.

The web jerked and I saw James coming up behind me. Fast. "What are you doing here, snot-rag?" he shouted.

I wasn't going to try to explain. It would waste time. James was not in a listening kind of mood.

I had to get to the garden tractor first. That was my only goal. I started down the other side of the web.

"Answer me!" James yelled. He flung his weight against the ropes and I almost lost my grip. I looked down. I was way too high up to think about jumping. Then I remembered the zip line.

"Later!" I grabbed the metal handle and rode the wire all the way to the ground. As soon as my toes hit the grass of the field, I started running again. I figured no one could have taken the course faster than James. But I was wrong.

Brynn was ahead of me. Tearing toward the best mower—the tractor with the bomb in it.

I focused my eyes on her back and put on speed. Lungs, legs, heart. All on fire. But I was gaining on her. I could almost grab her by the hood of her shirt. *Faster!*

She was veering to the side. She'd already reached the row of mowers. All I'd been seeing was her.

"Brynn, no!" I shouted as she climbed onto the seat of the tractor. "Stop!"

She didn't hesitate. She reached out and turned the ignition key.

I aimed myself at her and hurled myself into the air. The breath slammed out my body as I—as we—landed.

Brynn shoved at my shoulders. "What is wrong with you?"

I braced my body to take as much of the blast as possible.

A second later, it felt like the sun exploded.

## oose Threads

"I feel like I've been called to the principal's," Frank said. We'd made a bathroom stop on our way to meet with Veronica in the library.

"You mean that time you got the perfect attendance award?" I joked.

"I know it doesn't matter if we get booted. We solved the case. But I feel like I actually did get caught cheating," Frank admitted.

"Yeah. I don't like Brynn thinking I would do that," I said. "Just part of being ATAC sometimes . . . People think you're slime."

"Let's go get this over with," Frank told me.

"I've been thinking and thinking what to do with you boys," Veronica told us when we walked into the library. "I think I could make a case against you in court. You basically committed fraud by looking at the obstacle course in advance."

Oh, man. She was being even more hardcore than I thought.

"We had reason to believe that Mitch had sabotaged the mower—," I stopped myself, but it was too late.

"You shouldn't have known there were mowers, period," Veronica said. "You wouldn't have if you hadn't already begun cheating."

Oh, man. How would we get out of this without exposing ATAC to Veronica, a civilian?

"However, you did save Brynn's life," Veronica told Frank. "And for that reason, I'm willing to give you both a second chance."

We exchanged looks. So that meant we weren't off the show—we'd have to find a way to accomplish that part still, without raising too much suspicion. I guess we'd stick around a few days longer, then make our exit strategy. I had to admit, I didn't mind a little more time with Brynn.

Veronica held up one finger. "I will be watching you both extremely carefully, though. The slightest misstep will not be tolerated."

"You two are total heroes!" Olivia exclaimed at dinner that night.

"I can't believe what you found out about Mitch. He seemed so nice," said Mary.

James rolled his eyes and took the last ham sandwich from the plate in the middle of the dining room table. "Mitch was an idiot. He did what he did for twenty thousand—including robbing the bank?"

"Twenty grand is a lot of money," Olivia protested.

"It was twenty-five, actually," Joe corrected. "He spent five before he had to stash the rest."

"To go to jail," added Mikey.

"It would take a lot more to get me to kill," James insisted. "He should have, like, made some threats. Then told us he could take care of the problem for, let's say, twenty thou—collectable from the winner at the end of the show. Then he'd stop making the threats and get the cash."

"But Mitch had to kill somebody to get the job," I reminded James.

"Not a problem. See these guns?" He flexed his arms. "Veronica would have seen them and given me a job."

"I'm about to swoon myself," Brynn muttered. She absentmindedly ran her fingers over the bandage on the side of her neck. She'd taken a shard of flying metal from the tractor there, but it hadn't gone deep.

And Frank, he'd gotten some minor burns on his back and a few cuts and scrapes. It was pretty amazing, really.

"How long do you think Mitch will go to jail for?" Mikey asked.

"So long," said Frank. "With everything he did here, plus the bank robbery."

"I can't believe the cops had him in jail—and it wasn't even for the robbery." Bobby T shook his head. "I might have to blog about it."

"Putting him in jail for six months on the assault charge is basically what got him caught for the robbery and everything else," Frank said. "He hid the money here so it would be safe while he was in jail. That started the whole thing."

Veronica stepping into the room. "I have a surprise for you all." She sounded happy. That wasn't good.

"Recently I heard a story that touched my heart," she continued.

"Like the one about the little girl whose mommy was possessed by a demon?" said Mikey softly. I muffled a laugh with my napkin.

"It was a story about a young girl—a teenager like all of you," she continued. "But unlike any of you, this girl has experienced true poverty. She's gone to school hungry. She's gone to bed wearing a coat because her family couldn't afford enough heat. She knows the meaning of true deprivation."

Veronica beckoned to someone outside the door.

Had the girl been standing right there listening to Veronica's whole speech? Yikes.

A tall girl with close-cropped sandy hair walked into the room. "This is Gail Digby. Isn't she sweet?" Veronica wrapped her arm around Gail. "Winning a million dollars could change this girl's life in almost unimaginable ways."

She looked around like she wanted us to applaud or something. But that would be weird.

"I'll just take her upstairs and get her settled. I'm putting her in Kit's spot." Veronica walked Gail out of the room and shut the door behind them.

In about thirty seconds everyone was talking. I couldn't even keep the comments separate: "It's not fair to bring in someone new." "Veronica obviously wants her to win." "Veronica will make her win." "That speech made me want to hurl."

Things definitely didn't seem like they were going to start being peaceful at Deprivation House.

That night I woke up to the sound of a shrill scream. "This place," I muttered as I leaped out of bed and raced to the closest bathroom, where the screech had come from.

James was the only one inside. "That was you making that sound?"

"Yeah." He didn't even look embarrassed. "I was going to take a bath. I actually stepped into the bathtub to reach some soap, and I stepped on it." He jerked his chin toward the large, deep tub.

*What fresh insanity is this going to be?* I thought.

I moved closer and peered down.

"What's the deal?" asked Frank, rushing in.

"We have a new threat," I told him. Looks like our case wasn't closed after all. Good thing we hadn't left yet!

He joined me at the edge of the tub.

A blackbird lay at the bottom. Dead. Dead for a while, judging by the white maggots squirming in and out of its body.

"And I'm guessing that's not written in strawberry Jell-O," Frank said.

"I'm gonna have to agree," I added.

We both looked at the dripping red words smeared across the white porcelain: IT'S NOT OVER.

**The mystery continues in Book Two of the Murder House Trilogy, *House Arrest*. Here's a sneak peak!**

I glanced at the others in the kitchen doorway, realizing that Ripley wasn't among them. Neither was Mikey, like I said. Along with James, Bobby T, Brynn, and Olivia Gavener, I saw nerdy Hal Sheen, quiet homeschooler Mary Moore, and new-to-the-show Gail Digby.

That meant one other person was missing besides Ripley and Mikey. I couldn't think who it was at first. My brain was still half asleep.

I was still thinking when there was a loud shriek from elsewhere in the house.

Frank and I exchanged a look. "That sounded like it came from one of the girls' bedrooms," he said.

I nodded. "Let's go."

We raced back down the hall. I was in the lead as we burst into the room.

Ripley was standing there in front of the dresser. She was staring into the mirror, a look of horror on her face.

I could see why. Scribbled on her forehead in bloodred letters was the word MURDER.

Are you okay?" Joe rushed to Ripley's side.

"What happened?" I added. The others had followed us into the girls' bedroom. When they saw Ripley, there were a bunch of gasps and little cries of surprise.

"Whoa!" Bobby T had seemed a little quiet in the aftermath of Mouse Quest. Quiet for him, at least. Usually he talks nonstop. It's no wonder he started blogging—that way he can get it all out and nobody has to listen unless they want to. "Hold still, everyone," he added, sounding more like his usual self. "I gotta get my camera. This is so going on my blog!"

Ripley didn't seem to hear him. She was still staring at herself in the mirror. Her ice blue eyes were wide and anxious.

"Oh my God," Brynn moaned. When I glanced at her, she was clinging to the doorway. Her knuckles were white. "I thought we were done with this kind of thing when they caught Mitch."

Joe and I had thought that too. At least for a little while. We'd discovered that one of the production assistants was trying to scare us out of the house because he'd hidden the loot from an old bank robbery there.

"No way," James put in. "Mitch didn't leave that maggoty dead bird in the shower last night. He was long gone by then."

Yeah. No way had that bird flown in and died on its own. Case closed? Not quite. Joe and I might have caught one bad guy. But it seemed there was still another one in the house.

"Are you all right, Ripley?" I realized she still hadn't said anything. "Are you hurt?"

"Who did this?" Olivia demanded. "Ripley, did you write that on yourself? Because I have to tell you, it's not much of a joke."

Ripley rounded on her. "Don't be stupid," she snapped. "Do you really think I'd ruin my favorite Serge Lutens lipstick for some stupid joke? Grow up!"

Then she seemed to catch herself. She took several deep breaths.

"Sorry, Olivia," she said in a more normal tone. "I—I guess I'm just freaked out."

"Whatever." Olivia rolled her eyes. You don't have to be an undercover agent to see that Olivia isn't a Ripley fan.

Just then Bobby T returned. He started snapping pictures with his digital camera. I saw Ripley's jaw tighten for a second. But she didn't say anything. She just turned away and grabbed a tissue.

"Wait!" Bobby protested as she wiped at the sticky

red letters. "Let me get a few more angles!"

She didn't respond. Just kept rubbing until all that was left was a sort of maroonish blur.

That was a big step for her. I don't pay much attention to celebrity gossip myself—

## JOE

Joe here. I just have to say: understatement of the year. Dude, you didn't even know who Ripley Lansing *was* before we got this mission!

## FRANK

Okay, Joe. Enough. My point was, apparently Ripley is infamous for having meltdowns whenever the paparazzi get in her face. For her, *Deprivation House* wasn't about the money. She had plenty of that already. No, her appearance on the show was meant to be damage control for her out-of-control reputation. Sort of a kinder, gentler Ripley. Otherwise her parents were going to cut her off until she was thirty.

Just then another girl arrived in the doorway. She was yawning.

"What's going on?" she asked.

That was practically headline news. The late arrival's real name was Ann Sommerfeld. But everyone in the house called her Silent Girl. I guess it was her strategy for the game or something. I'd only heard her speak maybe twice in over a week. But I guess curiosity had gotten the best of her now.

Bobby T and Olivia started to explain. But Brynn cut them off.

"This is nuts!" she cried. "Why does this stuff keep happening? I'm starting to think this isn't worth it, million-dollar prize or not!"

Gail Digby nodded. "Girl, I am so with you." Her voice was shaking. "No cable, no AC—that stuff I'm used to. But this is just crazy!"

Nobody answered for a minute. What could we say? She had a point.

# Looking for a great read?

# MARGARET PETERSON HADDIX

# PENDRAGON

Bobby Pendragon is a seemingly normal fourteen-year-old boy. He has a family, a home, and a possible new girlfriend. But something happens to Bobby that changes his life forever.

## HE IS CHOSEN TO DETERMINE THE COURSE OF HUMAN EXISTENCE.

Pulled away from the comfort of his family and suburban home, Bobby is launched into the middle of an immense, interdimensional conflict involving racial tensions, threatened ecosystems, and more. It's a journey of danger and discovery for Bobby, and his success or failure will do nothing less than determine the fate of the world. . . .

**Coming Soon: Book Eight:** *The Pilgrims of Rayne*

**From Aladdin Paperbacks • Published by Simon & Schuster**